Mr.
CONfidence

Mr. Confidence

Rahiem Brooks

PRODIGY GOLD BOOKS

PHILADELPHIA * LOS ANGELES

MR. CONFIDENCE

A Prodigy Gold Book

Prodigy Gold E-book edition/May 2018

Prodigy Gold Paperback edition/May 2018

Library of Congress Catalog Card Number: 2017948708

Website: http://www.prodigygoldbooks.com

Author's e-mail: rbrooksbooks@yahoo.com

Editor: Locksie Locks

ISBN 978-1-939665-28-7

Published simultaneously in the US and Canada

PRINTED IN THE UNITED STATES OF AMERICA

Other books by Rahiem Brooks

The Bezel Brothers Series

Laugh Now

Die Later

Last Laugh

The Naim Butler Series

A Butler Christmas

A Butler Summer (June 2018)

The Ravonne Lemelle Series

Murder in Germantown

Murder in Love Park (November 2018)

Stand Alone Titles

Con Test

Mr. CONfidence

For

My family and friends.
All of them.

Mr. CONfidence

1

Don Juan Jackson walked through the State Correctional Institution Graterford gates. He carried nothing but humility and visions of a bright future. After serving a six-year prison bid for something stupid, angels sang around him and welcomed him back to the real world. He planned to exact the revenge that he had long desired. Sadly, he looked back at the 15 feet concrete wall that surrounded the prison and sighed. *Too bad I'll be back, and probably on death row*, he thought, and smiled. *Yeah, I'll definitely be back.*

The night before Don Juan had ripped up and trashed every letter, card, and picture from the dick-hungry-bitches that dropped him a line when he was knocking on the door to freedom. His mother didn't name him Don Juan for naught. From the moment that he popped out the depths of his mother's womb, she knew he would be a ladies man. God had not sent many chocolate coated babies with light brown eyes into the world to play the game. And Don Juan was an elite player with a new and improved set of rules. And they all desired to play with him.

He was 6'2", his bow-legged gait was visible across the prison parking lot. He strode confidently down the handicap ramp. *I'm back bitches*, he thought. To fight the sinister winter wind his right-hand man Lex had sent him a black mink baseball jacket, jeans, T-shirt, and black ski boots. All designer labels stolen for his pal's debut back into the world. At the bottom of the ramp, Lex stood there with a stupid grin on his face. He donned a diamond encrusted chain and cross that stopped at his belly button. A BMW limousine was parked behind him.

"My man," Lex said and gave Don Juan some dap and a hug. Lex was only 5'7", Puerto Rican and Black, and had the heart of a giant.

From inside the cab of the limousine, Don Juan heard a chorus of females.

"Good lookin' on the gear, bro. They gave me a check for three thousand that I had saved on my books. I gotta cash this bitch, and I can give you some bread back."

"Fuck dat. I'm up on some new shit. I got two bad bitches in the limo. They both want a shot of some fresh out of jail dick," Lex said, patting his homey on his back.

"Good, 'cause a brotha ready," Don Juan said, walking toward the limousine. He hadn't beat his dick in ninety days and was ready to fuck like a rock star.

Don Juan stuck his head into the limousine and saw his treats. One of them, a caramel babe with her hair pulled into a tight pony tail, and a truck load of ass hanging off the seat. She tapped the leather seat between her and an Asian woman.

"You can sit right here, daddy. Welcome home," she said and licked her lips.

Don Juan followed her command and then the limousine pulled off. He settled in his seat and the two woman snuggled next to him. The Asian woman placed her right hand on his dick. The Isley Brothers played in the background. He leaned in and kissed her ear before he whispered into it. "I always wanted to fuck an

Asian." In fact, while in prison, he vowed to fuck a woman of every race.

The Asian kissed Don Juan's cheek and left a cherry-red stain. "My father is black and my mother is Vietnamese. I have full dick sucking lips thanks to my father and a deep pussy thanks to my mother." She bent over and pulled up her form-fitting dress. She wasn't wearing panties. "This is a size 44. All ass and hips."

"Looks black to me," Lex said, winking at her.

"Exactly," she said. "And my name is Roneeka. How much more black can you get? Don't call me Asian."

"Oh, names," the woman with the ponytail interrupted. "I'm Brooke. Let's get you out of this jacket, Don Juan. What a fitting name for a man as fine as you." She tossed his jacket on the seat beside them.

Don Juan's biceps bulged from under his T-shirt. Roneeka touched him intimately all over his upper body. He immediately became erect.

"Fine and hard, Brooke," Roneeka said, running her hand up and down his dick. "What's this about a hard nine?"

"Or more," he replied and smiled. "What's these 36D?" He tickled her nipple.

"Double," she replied, smiling. "Or so. Who cares? Some man bought them."

Six long years had passed and Don Juan could not wait for this experience. Just the scent of a woman turned him on. Pretty or ugly, the fact that a female CO had a pussy had gotten him hard. It had been a difficult task not to masturbate those last three months, but he had to get a grip if he wanted to please a woman upon his release. He had been pleasuring himself no less than twice a day, and sometimes up to five. He knew that some woman loved cum, so he cheated himself to be sure that he was so backed up that he'd shoot a gallon the moment a woman touched him. Boy, did he have something in store for Brooke and Roneeka.

"I gotta ask this and I mean well. What were you in prison for, Don Juan?"

"Come on, Brooke," Lex said. "He tryinna fuck. He ain't tryinna talk. Tell her, Don Juan."

"Hold on, Lex," Don Juan said. "I've actually waited six long years to get a woman's perspective on this. Let me get a shot of this Patron first though, and then I'll be your storyteller."

2

SIX YEARS EARLIER

It was summer of 2003 and crack sales were at an all-time high for Don Juan. Despite that, he had two problems: a live-in girlfriend and mother to his baby girl, and another girl that was four months pregnant. Well, they two were one of his problems. The other was an overzealous rookie probation officer that had placed him under house arrest. That grand idea forced him to live under Sherry's roof, a gift for Sherry and his daughter, Trinity. After all, Sherry was the benefactor of his 24-hour, undivided attention. And with that honor, she was ready to hit the town and shake her ass. Hell, he was stuck in the house and not running the streets, so she did not have that to worry about. She told Don Juan that she was going out to Palmer's Night Club on Saturday to a Golden Girl party. Sherry further advised him that he was babysitting. *On house arrest, what the fuck else did he have to do,* she thought.

Saturday came and as planned Sherry, in a freak 'em dress, walked right out of the apartment door. She ignored Don Juan's pleas for her to change into something more respectable. Many of his boys would be there, putting her in line to be hit on by some lame with a hard-on to say, "I fucked Don Juan's bitch." When his cell phone rang and he saw Saleena's name on the caller ID, he knew she wanted to start trouble, because she was not allowed to call him when Sherry wasn't at work.

Reluctantly, he answered the phone. "What's up, baby?" he said cheerfully. His smile could not have been phonier.

"Don't baby me just 'cause that bitch ain't there down ya throat."

"Where are you? I can't really hear you?" Don Juan asked. He heard her perfectly fine but was prepared to hang up on her and pretend that he had lost the call.

"I'm at Palmer's. In the bathroom. I'm tying up my hair. When I am done, I'm gone beat that bitch Sherry's ass. ASAP."

"No! Yo, Leena. Don't do any dumb shit. You're pregnant."

"Fuck dat. All that shit that bitch talked when she was prego over these Bell Atlantic airwaves. Oh, hell to the fucking no, bitch. That hoe had the wrong one. I told her that I was beating her ass on sight. And guess what Don-fucking-Juan? That bitch is in my sight. I'mma whoop this bitch ass and send her right back to your tired ass, fucked up."

"I wasn't tired when I was slamming this pipe all in you. Matter of fact, a few times I put ya lazy ass to sleep. You're going to get what you're looking for if you fuck with her, Leena."

"Is that a threat, you punk ass, sucka. I'll call ya PO and get ya pretty ass locked up. I shoulda known you were lame."

"Bitch, you're going mad. You were just trying to come up in this crib and get ya back blown out this morning when she was at work. And now you wanna get me locked up."

"You're right. It's been a change of plans mutha fucka." She hung the phone up.

* * *

Forty minutes later, Don Juan was stretched out on the sofa with Trinity spread across his chest when Sherry traipsed into the door. She was quiet and tossed her keys into a dish on the table by the front door.

"Mommie's home," Don Juan said and raised his baby into the air. Trinity smiled and held out her tongue in laughter.

Don Juan noted that Sherry didn't look like she had been in a fight.

She walked into the bedroom, kicked off her shoes, shimmied out of her dress, and then walked to the dresser. She looked into the mirror and saw Don Juan at the door holding Trinity.

"That bitch."

"What bitch?" Don Juan asked as if he had no clue.

Sherry turned around and slapped the stupidity right out of him. Nothing angered her more than him acting like a saint.

"Your other baby momma is on her way here to get her ass kicked. You know she assured me that she knew where I lived. And now, I assure you that if that bitch comes here, I am going to demolish that trick and send her on her way. And your silly ass will be right behind her, so pack ya shit."

"You know I have this ankle monitor on, Sherry. That woman is just mad that I live with you."

"I don't care. Why the fuck does she know where I live and work? You planned on fucking that bitch in my home in front of my child this morning. That ugly bitch."

"Look—," Don Juan was interrupted by a loud blare of car horns. Sherry tried to push past him, but he grabbed her. "Don't take your ass out there, Sherry."

She snatched away from him. "Loser, pack ya shit. That's what you do," she said, walking right out of the apartment door.

From the second story window, Don Juan looked down to a car full of women. He shot a .40-cal bullet into the air and warned the crowd below. "If any of you touch her, I'll kill you bitches right from this window. Go home!"

"You ain't killing shit," Saleena yelled at him.

Bolting out of the complex front door came Sherry. She raced down the stairs, leading to the pavement as she yanked off her T-shirt. In only a sports bra, Sherry two-pieced the hell out of Saleena, who lost her balance, but managed to throw back a wild punch that hit nothing.

"Let 'em fight fair," Don Juan yelled out the window.

"I'mma get my brother to see you about shooting at me, pussy," one of Saleena's loud-mouthed friends yelled up to him.

Don Juan ignored her. Despite the situation, he remained calm. He heard cries from the baby's crib and raced over to her. He put her pacifier back into her mouth, patted her back, and then headed back to the window in time to see Sherry pounding Saleena's head on the pavement. *God, she's going to kill her*, Don Juan thought, as he ran over and grabbed the baby. He then ran out to break up the skirmish. He didn't give a damn about any electronic monitoring device.

Don Juan used his free arm and pulled Sherry off Saleena just as the Philadelphia finest pulled up. *Fuck!* Both officers were girls-in-blue. Just what he needed, more woman on the scene with power over his life.

"Sherry, go into the apartment now," he barked at her, but it was too late. To Saleena, he said, "You asked for this, and you better not hit my daughter."

"What's going on here?" Officer Dorsey asked and popped a wad of gum in her mouth. "We were told that shots were fired."

"That's the truth officer," Saleena screamed, "he tried to kill me for fighting his baby mom. Yeah, him right there." She was pointing.

"Officer, she's drunk, came here, and assaulted my BM. She followed her from the club." Don Juan was calm.

"Give me my child. I ain't your fuckin' BM," Sherry said, pulling the baby from his arms.

"That clown shot at me and that bitch assaulted me, officer," Saleena said. "I want both of they asses locked up and yes, I wanna press charges."

"Right now, ma'am, I have you all for mutual combat and disorderly conduct. I suggest that you stop running this you want someone locked up bullshit, 'cause you'll be going, too," Officer McSimpson said with a sassy hand on her hip.

"Let me talk to you sir," Officer Dorsey said, and then walked toward the police car. She said, "Tell me what happened."

"I am innocent this time, ma'am," he said, batting his long eye lashes.

"Let me be frank for a minute. Off the record. I don't like dick," the officer said and poked his chest with her nightstick forcing him to stumble backward. "Not even on black ass men, with pretty eyes. So don't try to charm me. What the fuck happened? And if I hear a sentence, fragment, or comment that is off base, I am hauling ya ass to the 35th."

"My girlfriend, Sherry, just had our daughter and wanted to go out. So, she did and bumped into Saleena at Palmer's. I was hitting Saleena while Sherry was pregnant. Sherry came home from the club and tells me that Saleena threatened to come here to fight. She came and they fought. One of Saleena's friends shot a gun into the air and told me that I better not come out of the apartment, but I did. I called the police before I came down to break it up. That's when you pulled up." He prayed none of that sounded off base. Picture, Don Juan, calling the police.

"Who had the gun?"

"When the sirens were close the girl with the gun ran off. It was about ten cars out here before your sirens were close," Don Juan said as other policemen pulled onto the scene. "I swear I can handle Sherry. Please don't arrest her, she was only protecting herself. Just have them all leave, ma'am."

"Now, you wanna tell me how to do my job," the officer told him, then called her partner who was writing on a note pad and talking to other officers. "Go sit over there," Officer Dorsey told Don Juan, pointing to the curb.

"It's wet," he said, complaining. "It was raining."

"There or the back of the car."

"Say no more. I'll be on the curb."

"That's what the fuck I thought," Officer McSimpson said.

"These silly bitches are fighting over some dick. I don't feel like writing this up for him to persuade them both not to come to court on each other. I don't wanna waste my time," Officer Dorsey said.

"That's all I have. I'll threaten them wenches and you finish with him," Officer McSimpson replied.

"Deal," Officer Dorsey said, and then signaled for Don Juan and Sherry to rejoin her. "Look, it's 1:30 in the morning and you have an infant out here in this wet weather. I could haul you both to jail and take the baby to DHS. You're out here fighting tells me that you really don't give a damn about your baby. What kinda mother does this? But I won't do that. And he's on house arrest. The last thing he needs is this. You two go back inside, kiss and makeup. I guarantee if I come back both of you are going to jail. Let me talk to him a minute." Sherry walked away and into the apartment. Then Officer Dorsey said, "She's going to kick you out, so I suggest that no matter how good the makeup sex is tonight, Monday you better move. Or the moment that she gets pissed at you for something as small as leaving the toilet seat up at night, you're going to jail."

3

PRESENT DAY

"That's some bullshit," Brooke said, massaging Don Juan's shoulders. The limousine bounced down I-76 en route to Philadelphia.

"How'd you actually get in jail?" Roneeka asked, rubbing his rock hard, washboard stomach.

"Saleena called my PO and told her that I shot a gun. So my dumb ass PO locked me up and at my hearing, Saleena cried on the witness stand about her miscarriage that I caused and that I shot at her. The stupid judge said that if the standard of proof was beyond a reasonable doubt that he would have to acquit me. But because it was only preponderance of the evidence, he found me guilty of violating my probation. So he took the probation back and gave me 3-6 years in jail, which I maxed out because of fighting and being caught with a cell phone and gambling."

"And that the same thing that happened to Meek Mill?"

"Yup."

"That's fucked up," Roneeka said.

"I know," Don Juan told her. "You should suck my dick and make it better." He unbuckled his pants and slipped his jeans and boxers around his ankles. He kicked his boots off as he hoisted Brooke's tits right out her strapless dress. He then kicked his jeans and boxers off. He stretched his legs out and opened them for Roneeka to kneel between them.

After a thirty minute ride of limo sex, Roneeka told Don Juan, "Welcome home."

4

The limousine finally pulled onto Wayne Avenue in Happy Hollow in the Germantown section of Philadelphia. Lex had the driver pull over in front of Charlie B's Bar. He slipped the driver a $200 tip and gave the girls $500 each. He, then, had the driver take Brooke and Roneeka home. Don Juan and Lex watched the limo pull off and was glad to be back in their part of town. They were in front of the bar that made the Happy Hollow pop. The one thing that Don Juan noticed was that the strip had not changed at all while he was in the joint. At one in the afternoon, the regular neighborhood hoes were out and barely bundled up for the winter weather.

"Listen," Lex said, walking toward a BMW 745. He popped the trunk. "I got this new iPhone for you. And here's a cheap Cricket prepaid phone, too. Get in, we need to talk and ride. Oh, this laptop is for you, also."

"I gotta see my kid and my peoples, dawg," Don Juan said, as Lex pulled off.

He headed north on Wayne Avenue.

"I know, but the game out here has changed. I gotta put you down with what I am doing. The drug game is some shit, my dude. Everyone has turned into rats. It's hot as a mutha fucka out here. No one is to be trusted. Not even the so-called king pin, or your close homey. Stupid men are laying down bodies and bragging about that shit. As soon as someone gets knocked by the feds, their homey's are telling and cutting deals. The phone towers are tracking people's movements. You lie and say you were in ATL, but phone towers put ya black ass at the crime scene. Don't carry a phone registered to you to do any dirt. Don't call any of your family on a throwaway phone, either. Do not under any circumstances take a phone as a gift. It may be bugged. And don't buy one on the street or find one on the street, as you never know what has been done with it. Hell, don't mutha fuckin' borrow one to make a call.

Look in the glove compartment," Lex said and cued Jay-Z's album to play in the background.

A gun was stuffed in the glove compartment, along with some cash.

"Pull out the envelope, too," Lex said, pulling into the Burger King parking lot at Wayne and Chelten Avenues. "Open it."

Inside the envelope was a key ring with the Range Rover insignia on one of the keys, and a house key. Lex continued, "In your lap is a new gun for your protection and $20,000. That black Range over there is a 2007 and it's paid for. It's yours. The other key is for a one car garage, three bedrooms home. It's partially furnished and up there on Mount Pleasant in Mount Airy. The address is on the key ring. All this shit is yours. You don't owe me shit. All I ask is that you follow the new rules of the drug game."

"Lex, I grew up with you since we were knee high. You pushin' bricks now." Don Juan was confused. *Where the fuck this dude get all this shit from?*

"Naw, I'm on some serious white collar shit," Lex said as a Cadillac Escalade that sat on 24's, pulled into the drive-thru with a banging system. "That's Popz, a sucka from Newark, but he got the best work Uptown.

He gets a pass 'cause he's Big Sam's long lost son. And he has the best prices."

"I'm not sure this drug game is for me anymore. The way you put it, you can't trust anyone. After doing six years, homey, I ain't tryinna go back."

"That's why you're following the new drug rules."

"What are they? After jail, I don't want to follow any rules at all."

"That's the thing. There are no rules if you not in the game. The new rule is simple, don't get into the drug game. What you just said seems like you want a 9-5. Know that all crimes lead to prison. At least potentially. If you think that you're going to escape, you better be very slick or a rat. Otherwise, you're going to jail like everyone else. Philly PD is desperate out here. And the feds are locking up dope feigns."

"I know, man. Dudes in the joint talking about the police had crack heads lie on them to get out of possession charges. They lying in affidavits and all."

"So, you know. If you get into the drug game you will be hit. I got your back. And by the way, Roneeka's mom is a lawyer that used to be a federal prosecutor. And, yes, I am hitting that on the low." Lex dug into his wallet and tossed Don Juan a business card. "That's her card. You get into anything call her. And be sure to call her tomorrow to set up a retainer."

"Aiight. Dig this. Christmas is in eight days. I gotta get my daughter straight. Party all through New Years with my folks and then I'mma have to get at a dolla."

"I gotta go to New York tonight for business. You should come. I'm meeting with some people at the Soul Cafe that I do business with. Afterwards, we can grab a hotel, party all night and shop all up and down Fifth Avenue tomorrow. You can get the baby some Gucci shit."

"Aiight cool. What time are we out?"

"Meet me at Amtrak 'bout seven. We can grab the 7:30 Acela. Go up to Neiman's at King of Prussia Mall and grab something to wear. The cafe is for the rich black folk, so dress accordingly."

5

Chelten Avenue was a four-block strip of retailers, jewelers, banks, and other emporiums. Don Juan drove down the strip and wondered, what the fuck had gotten into Lex. Six years ago, they were both 22, and Don Juan had all the answers as the ringleader. Lex was the dumb, young bull, who was likely to have a battery placed in his back to do something dumb. But that had changed. At 28, Lex was running the show. Don Juan pulled over, parked at a check cashing place, and had the mindset that he was ready to fall in line. Which line, he had no clue, but he was born to get money. What he did not want was any part of the jail's chow or commissary line, as far as that went.

Don Juan parked and hopped out the Range with all eyes on him. He waved at a few hoes that he had bagged before he had left. Outside of the check cashing place, a man sold bootleg CDs, DVDs, and socks. Don Juan bought $100 worth of rap and R&B CDs that he had missed out on. He then went inside the check cashing place.

Knowing that Sherry planned to hit him for child support, like every other hood rat, he had the clerk photocopy the check, before he had her convert it into a money order. He had $23,000, and giving Sherry $3,000 for the baby was a drop in the bucket.

* * *

Twenty minutes later, Don Juan was in the Summerville area parked on Price Street. Sherry lived in a cute row house with her fiancé, but as long as his bloodline lived there, he was welcomed. He called Sherry on his cell phone, and she answered on the third ring.

"Sherry, it's me," he said just like the good ole times.

"Boy, don't make me call that prison and have that counselor put your fucking ass in the hole for having a cell phone. Now, I asked you not to fucking call me. I'm getting married, and you can write Trinity. The child that I am out here taking care of."

"Sherry, look out your front window." He was calm. Don Juan heard the phone drop, and several seconds later, he watched her peak out the living room curtain.

A few more seconds later, her man was on the line. "Look here, dude..."

Don Juan cut him off smooth. He wasn't trying to hear any bullshit. "Dig this homey, I ain't got no problems with you. I just want to take care of mines. Don't get in my way, cuz."

"You're in my way."

"Just put Sherry on, so we can arrange my visits with my daughter."

Don Juan had the desire to shoot up that entire house. He did not want any trouble and had not planned to start any. He was a cannon that didn't like his buttons pushed because he would detonate. The front door opened and Sherry stepped onto the porch with her man right behind her. Don Juan had heard that she had had another baby, but her shape remained intact. *I don't want her, though. And this weirdo marching*

down the steps behind her better keep his mouth shut, or I'm
pushing his wig back.

Don Juan stepped out of the Range Rover and
showed off how tall and well-built he had become. He
wasn't the skinny man that Sherry or her fiancé
expected.

"I'm going to make this quick," Don Juan said and
held out the money order. "There's $3,000. I'm asking
you not to get the courts involved in our business. I will
take care of Trinity. I don't want to come here, but all I
ask is that you drop her off at my mom's house or let
my sister pick her up when I want to see her, or she
wants to see me. Don't let no man touch my kid, and
she damn sure better not ever call another man, dad.
You got all that, ma?" Don Juan asked staring at
Sherry's fiancé.

"Yeah, I heard you," she said with a nasty attitude.

"Where is she now?"

"It's Thursday. School, where else?"

"Right, she's in first grade over there at Pastorious.
Don't look all stupid. You don't think I kept tabs on
mine. Thanks for not answering my letters, but I have
copies, so she'll know that daddy thought about her."

"OK, that's enough," the fiancé said.

Don Juan, with venom in his eyes, turned and stepped deep into the man's face. He wasn't scared of the gun that the man pulled out and put in his face.

"Shoot, homie," Don Juan said and smiled. A wicked smile indeed. The man blinked. "You're not brave enough. Besides," Don Juan said and stepped back. "Sherry would be the state's star witness against you."

"Come on, Rob, he ain't worth it," Sherry said, tugging his shirt.

"Yeah, Rob," Don Juan said, mimicking her. He backed away and then turned around. "I'd like to see my baby on Saturday around six. Drop her at my mom's house," he said with them looking at his back. He hopped into the truck, rolled down the passenger window, and then said, "And, Rob, you better get rid of that cop gun." He blasted *Duffle Bag Boys* by Player's Circle and Lil Wayne, as he rolled away.

6

By 9:15 p.m. Lex and Don Juan strolled outside of Pennsylvania Station in New York City and emerged onto 7th Avenue along Madison Square Garden. They looked debonair and suave in suits, chinchilla, and cashmere scarfs. Two Philadelphians dressed to shut down The Big Apple. Don Juan donned a Philip Treacy fedora with a 16-inch feather that he had bought at Neiman's earlier that day.

After a short ride in a Lincoln Continental, they were dropped off at the Soul Cafe on West 42nd Street. At the entrance to the theater-styled cafe, they heard the sultry Jazmine Sullivan singing *Lions, Tigers, and Bears*. The live band under her voice was delightful.

"So you wanna tell me what kind of business are you on, homie?" Don Juan asked as they sat on stools at a mahogany bar. He told the bartender, "I'll have a double vodka with a glass of coke on the side."

"I'll have the same, but with orange juice," Lex said.

"Can I bring you menus?"

"No, thank you," Lex replied and the bartender stepped off.

"Dude, you gon' answer my question?"

"I gotta handle some business."

"You told me that."

Lex pondered a moment. He wanted to put Don Juan down but didn't know how much that he could reveal at once. He finally said, "I'm about to buy one hundred American Express customer profiles." Lex paused and gripped his cocktail. He coolly took a sip and then went on. "They bought your car and the crib. I also have a connect for fake, but very passable ID's. I take over a person's identity, get mortgages or car notes in their names, and pay the shit off. I then sell it to some street thugs."

"One of my cellmates in jail was into that type of shit. What I want to know is if you pay everything off, how do you make a real profit?"

"Easy, my boy," Lex replied and clapped along with the audience to conclude Jazmine's set. "I open bank accounts, too, and funnel through it counterfeit checks. Speaking of checks, where's that state check? I wanna rob them bastards for keeping you in jail." He laughed lightly and sipped his drink again.

"I cashed it."

"Damn, I could have duplicated it, and robbed them bitches."

"I have a copy of it."

Lex furrowed his eyebrow. He was confused. "What the hell did you copy it for?"

"'Cause I broke Sherry off. I changed it to a money order, but I copied it, so she couldn't claim that it was illegal money. I don't trust that bitch, cuz."

"That was smart," he said, staring at the stage. "There's my connect."

"Where?"

"One the stage with the mic in her hand. She 'bout to blow like Fantasia. She goes to the Fashion Institute of Technology, but works part-time at an Amex office in the financial district."

"I know you hitting that? That's a bad bitch, Lex."

"She's strictly pussy, and claims that she has never had a dick."

"Damn, ask her can I watch."

Lex ignored the question. "When she's done, you're going to move to one of those candlelit tables. She will come there, and I am going to pass her an envelope after a brief conversation. At that point, you head to the door and grab a taxi. Let the driver run the meter, but hold him until I get there."

* * *

At 11:30 p.m., Lex hopped into the taxi, and told the driver," The Pierre, sir."

"What's the Pierre?" Don Juan asked as the taxi pulled off. "And you look empty-handed."

"Watch and learn, homie?"

Ten minutes later, they pulled in front of the grand Pierre Hotel on Fifth Avenue. Lex paid the driver and they walked under the white canopy to the hotel's entrance. They were greeted by a bellman that opened the door.

"Welcome to the Pierre," a front desk clerk said to Lex. She was a waif, Belgian woman, named Helga.

"I have a reservation," he said and pulled out his fake ID. "David Van Dyke."

Helga tapped her computer and said, "It seems that your room was canceled, and unfortunately we are sold out. There is a package here for you, though."

"I'll take that, ma'am, but could you call around to a few of the other five star hotels and locate me another room, please."

"Certainly, Mr. Van Dyke."

Lex walked over to Don Juan and listened to his entire conversation with Helga coming from Don Juan's cell phone. He had recorded them.

"This phone does a lot of things," Don Juan said. "I have it set up to record with the touch of a button, and I can't wait to record the sound of a bitch slurpin' on this pipe."

"Our reservation was canceled," Lex said, and then tapped his bag. "Got the profiles, though."

"So, what are we going to do?"

"I got the clerk over there finding another hotel."

"Good, I'm going to chill outside and hop on one of these apps to find some freak bitches that are trying to come to the hotel while you take care of that."

Lex walked back to the hotel clerk and pulled off his lambskin gloves. His palms perspired with the anticipation of putting the profiles to use. He was antsy like a kid a few weeks before Christmas. Lex slipped his thumb under the triangle metal clasp and pulled the attaché open. He pulled out an 8x10 sheet of paper and scanned the profile of Edmond Craft, a 37-year-old, dentist from Rochester, Minnesota.

"Pardon, Mr. Van Dyke. It seems that none of the hotels as far away as the World Trade Center district have rooms available. Would you like me to try Brooklyn or even Newark airport?"

"No, that'll be fine. Do you have a listing of...Never mind," he said and grinned. He had almost asked if she had known the next time an Amtrak train would leave New York for Philadelphia. That would've given her a lead for the cops in the event that they questioned the hotel about him. He doubted that would happen, but he couldn't have that. He bid the clerk a good night and left the hotel.

Out on Fifth Avenue, Don Juan said into his phone, "Those are all jail flicks on my Facebook page. You gotta come to the hotel to see if I really live up to the name, Don Juan...Come on, ma...Hold up." Walking down the street, he put the phone to his side and whispered to Lex, "Where we staying at?"

"Uptown."

"Come on with this uppity Uptown/Downtown bullshit."

"Taxi," Lex yelled to a passing yellow cab. To Don Juan, he said, "We're going home. There are no hotels up this bitch."

"This is New York. It has to be. Besides I have this bitch I met on this dating app that I am trying to fuck."

"Go to her spot," Lex said, climbing into the taxi. "Hit it and we can make a 3 a.m. train out of here."

"Come on, man," Don Juan said with a frown. He seemed disappointed. There was no way that he was going to be in New York by himself.

"What, man. She's on an app at midnight. She wants to fuck for sure. You ain't forget the game. You lost your brains in the jail. Give me the phone, DJ."

"Oh, you're a ladies man, huh? Take the phone, man. Let me see your work," Don Juan said, passing Lex his cell phone.

7

Under the night darkness, Don Juan and Lex emerged from the subway train station. They stared at the Mets Shea Stadium with the backdrop of a low-income housing projects. They posted up under the cover of a bus stop and Don Juan called Monica. She again told him that she lived two blocks from the train station and that she would meet them on the corner of her block.

"This shit better not be a setup. And she better be as bad as her Facebook flicks," Don Juan said as they walked down the street.

"Man, we up in Queens looking like meal tickets. You better hope that we don't get robbed."

"We ain't got any bread on us."

"DJ, I got 100 profiles on me. Do you know how much these are worth?"

"Fuck dat." Don Juan didn't care about any damn profiles. All he knew about was selling white girl. Even after his cellie had told him how sweet the fraud game was, Don Juan was not about to steal the white man's money.

"You're speaking from stupidity," Lex said, smiling. "But, I'mma show you, though."

"Naw, let me show you about pulling a bad girl," Don Juan said, pointing up the street. "You can see that ass on her from here."

"Damn, she does have cakes, if that's her." Lex agreed. "You sure that's her?"

"Yeah, blue jeans and a short leather jacket."

"That's her alright," Lex said with her close enough to hear him.

"Yeah, it's me," Monica said, smiling. She had a perfectly bronzed complexion, white teeth, and a body that other women bought. "Y'all wasn't playing, huh?"

"Naw, ma," Don Juan said. "We don't play. So we gon' head back to your spot. Smoke and drink." He held up a bottle of Ciroc that he grabbed from a 24-hour bodega in Manhattan.

"It's whateva," Monica said with her deep New York accent. "Let me see some ID."

"What?" Don Juan and Lex said in unison. They were chuckling.

"You're kidding, right?" Don Juan asked, "I just got out earlier today. I don't have one." He flashed her a coy smile because he wanted to fuck her badly.

"I believe you," she said and turned to face Lex with her hand out. He passed her his wallet. Into her cellphone, she said, "Yeah, Shay. I met them two Philly dudes. The Don Juan guy is the one on Facebook, but I have his homie ID. His name is David Van Dyke, but he's a black, light skinned brotha wit' pretty hair. His address is 6151 Reeves Road, Rochester, Minnesota. If I don't call you by 10 in the morning, go after this guy." She hung up with her own answering machine, handed Lex his wallet, and then told them, "My sister Shay's husband is a cop, so if you try anything she's going to get him on the case." It was a lie, but she used it and it had kept her safe when meeting random men in the past.

"If I was about to commit a crime, I'd care, ma," Don Juan said.

"You gotta little smart ass mouth. Let's get outta this cold New York air," Monica said.

I need to put something in your mouth, Don Juan thought.

"Hold on. Let me see some ID, you could be a killer," Lex said seriously. She gave him, a no-this-man-didn't-look, and he smiled. "Just fuckin' with you."

They all burst into laughter and then walked down a few brownstones. The front of Monica's crib looked like the set from the Cosby Show. The house had been broken into apartments. Inside the vestibule reeked of a scented candle. Monica opened her apartment door and treated them to a glimpse of an artsy African-power themed living room. The room was covered with a multitude of autumn colors. A staircase was on the far wall that led down to the basement, which had been transformed into a large bedroom and lounge area.

When they reached the bottom of the stairs, Monica offered them a seat in front of a wall mounted plasma TV. On the glass table was ten weed-filled Dutches inside a candy jar and two candy dishes filled with an assortment of pills from Ecstasy to Viagra. About six feet away was a bedroom area filled with pink and black furniture and bedding.

"You got a lot of candy," Don Juan said, pulling a Dutch from the candy jar. "And I got a sweet tooth."

"That's how we do it in Queens, baby," Monica said, plopping on a large chaise. "So, why y'all fly and shit?" she asked, tossing Don Juan a lighter.

Before he answered, Lex said, "I'mma go upstairs and make a few calls. Let you get to know my homie a little better. Remember, he got out of jail this morning."

8

At 11 a.m. the next morning, the sound of a headboard banging the wall and the intimate moans of Monica was heard through the train car. Don Juan and Lex smiled as the older woman behind them turned her head in shame, pretending that she had never heard lovemaking. Don Juan had recorded himself having sex with Monica.

When the train reached 42nd Street and Broadway, they disembarked the train and took a taxi over to 8th Avenue. In front of Madison Square Garden, Don Juan expressed that he wasn't ready to leave without shopping. Lex walked away from the bus terminal and told him that not only were they about to shop, but he would turn him onto his first lick.

"You saw Transformers while in jail, right?"

"Yeah, that was a good movie."

"While you were in the basement pounding that beautiful ass, I was up on the sofa planning your transformation into Mr. Anwar Muhammad," Lex said and passed a stolen profile to Don Juan. "You could transform into him easily."

"Two things. One, I don't look like a Middle Easterner."

"You will when we go and buy you a kufi and Muslim garb. Just think of it as a costume."

"I am not an actor. And two, I am not with this white collar shit, homie."

"Come on wit' this bullshit. You'd rather go sling some dope. That's just what you're used to, I get that. But you gotta look at the time factor. All I'm asking you to do is go to a few department stores to open instant credit accounts to buy whatever you want. Look at it this way, all that shit you wanted to go buy, you can, and keep the cash in your pocket. A win-win."

They looked at each other for a moment and then Don Juan shook his head.

"I thought, you'd see it my way," Lex said, smiling. "Let's get busy."

They walked along 8th Avenue and Lex stopped in front of a cheap motel on 43rd Street between 8th and 9th Avenues. He walked into the lobby with Don Juan in tow and approached the front desk. He told a sloppy fat man behind a bulletproof glass that he was there to see Roxy. Lex was directed to room 417 and walked toward an elevator.

On the elevator, Don Juan asked, "Who the fuck is Roxy? You stopped in the middle of our business to come here and fuck? Nice."

"Hell naw, DJ. Ms. Roxy is going to make your first fake ID. Where's Muhammad from?"

"You act like I know."

"Look at the damn profile, man. Stop the dumb act. That's why Sherry busted you upside the head." Both men chuckled. "I ain't acting dumb, bro. He's from Jacksonville, Florida."

"Use your cell phone for something other than recording, and Google that city. Find a college in that area and read all about it."

"And, what the fuck is that for?" Don Juan asked as Lex knocked on the door to room 417.

"'Cause we 'bout to meet my ID connect. She's going to give you a Florida ID and a college ID too. It's gon' cost you $300."

"Me?"

"Yes, you. You're about to make 10 to 20 times that."

* * *

Back on 43rd Street, Lex and Anwar Muhammad, the Muslim from Jacksonville, who attends Jacksonville University walked towards 8th Avenue. Lex flagged down a taxi and had the driver take them to an Islamic clothing store. When they got there, Lex ran into the store and grabbed the rest of Anwar's costume. He returned to the taxi and told the driver, "Bloomingdale's. 59th and Lexington." To Don Juan, he said, "You got 'bout 15 blocks to change."

The relatively short trip took twenty minutes in the thick Manhattan traffic. When they hopped out the taxi, Don Juan could not believe what he planned to do. Despite the difference in prison time between identity theft and pushing crack, he was scared. The idea of taking what he termed "the white man's money" scared him, but so did peer pressure, perhaps. There was no way that he wanted to back out on a smooth lick that afforded him the goods for free, and it did not involve gunplay or a violent police chase. Dressed in a black dashiki, Gucci boots with the signature red, black and green icon print around the top, and a red, black and green *kufi*, Don Juan planned to do it all to become, Mr. Anwar Muhammad.

9

Stylish sales associates and aggressive New York shoppers zipped about Bloomingdale's in search of gifts and bargains. Considering Don Juan had a strong desire to load up on Christmas gifts for Trinity, he went to the kid's section to buy her things. He had six years to makeup and Christmas was the perfect time to be completely forgiven. *How much would it take to spoil a six-year-old back into my good graces?*

Lex posed as a fashion stylist and paraded around the children's department selecting piece by piece. Don Juan had to call his mother to confirm Trinity's sizes. He hoped that everything that he stole was to her liking.

At the checkout register, fifty minutes later, Don Juan neatly laid a load of clothing on the counter and a very tall woman with long hair snatched them up. The Friday before Christmas was extremely busy and she was getting customers in and out of her way. She scanned all of Don Juan's items, and then said, "Your total is $1,927.16. But you can save 10% today if you open a Bloomingdale's charge account."

The statement was music to Lex's ears.

Don Juan's, too. "I can do that," he said to her, giving her a sly grin.

The sales associate was grateful because, for every charge account that she opened, she received a $20 bonus on her paycheck. "I'll need a state ID and a credit card," the woman said, as she passed him a paper application.

Don Juan carefully filled out the application and disguised his real style of writing. He followed Lex's strict directions with respect to remembering every fact from the profile and recording it on the application. A good memory and quick thinking were paramount to this paper chase. A little more than street smarts was required. Don Juan completed the application and passed it back to the sales lady along with his ID, but without the required credit card.

Don Juan told her, "I had expected to use cash today, and intentionally left my credit cards at home." He pulled out a wad of cash, and continued, "I never expected to open an account, but I do have an American Express, though."

Good fucking job, Lex thought. Recklessly, he had forgotten to tell Don Juan about his lack of a credit card. But Don Juan handled that smoothly.

The saleswoman processed the application and then told him that, he was approved with a spending limit of $3,500. She completed the sale, gave Don Juan a receipt and temporary Bloomingdale's card, and offered him a good day.

When they were away from the saleswoman, Don Juan said, "I didn't even need the college ID and the other Jacksonville bullshit."

"You did. You gotta be on point. Suppose she was from Jacksonville. Worse, a JU college grad, and began to engage you about the city and college?"

"I would have told her...Hold on, where are we going?" Don Juan asked as Lex led him up an escalator and deeper into the store. He wanted out of there.

"The men's department. You have about $1,500 more in credit. But finish telling me about what you would have told her."

"Oh, that I just moved there and hadn't really gotten around yet."

"That's some aiight bullshit, but trust me, if you can engage a sales associate in a conversation about their hometown it takes their mind off the task at hand: paying attention to the crime you are committing right before them. Before you know it, they've sold you 5-, 10-, 20-thousand dollars' worth of merchandise." They stepped off the escalator. "I want you to get a lot of accessories up here. Briefcase, attaché, wallets, ties, that sort of shit. Tell the clerk it's for your father and father-in-law if asked."

"I am Muslim, remember? I don't celebrate Christmas."

"You're American, though. Of course, you do," Lex said, chuckling.

* * *

Four hours later, walking down the stairs at Penn Station, Don Juan carried bags from a few of New

York's lavish stores: Bergdorf Goodman, Macy's Saks Fifth Avenue, Nordstrom and Barney's New York. He had an innate bit of confidence, but what he had done had given a renewed sense of arrogance. And it was such an easy crime to commit. No planning. Not much risk. Just simply being himself got him the goods. He was a go-getting money maker that would have sold crack to pay for the $30,000 worth of things he had stolen. But walking down another flight of stairs, after his heist, he thought that selling crack was the dumbest thing on the planet. Far as he knew, his cash purchase days were over.

Why not?

Don Juan and Lex settled into seats on an Amtrak Acela in the executive car headed for Philadelphia. A conductor approached them and they both requested cocktails and cheesecake danishes. Don Juan needed a drink. He always saw himself as smooth, but to pull off the New York stunt had his spirits over the moon.

The train exited the tunnel entering New Jersey like a bullet flying in a gunfight. Both men were quiet, and simply thinking, only being interrupted by the vibrations of Lex's cell phone. He answered the call, quoted some numbers, and then hung up.

"Trying to make about 30 G's?" Lex asked Don Juan plainly. Don Juan did not respond. He looked dumbfounded and furrowed his brows in confusion. "All you have to do is act like Anwar Muhammad again. This time in one of those luxuriant suits with one of those briefcases you just bought," Lex said, smiling.

10

A little later, Lex picked up his car from 30th Street Station and then drove to his home in Northeast Philadelphia. His neighbors—a policeman on one side and a fireman on the other—regarded him as a quiet, reserved, coy young man headed in the right direction. Lex was more likely headed to a comfy federal prison to join his favorite rap artist, Clifford Harris, Jr. He walked up the long walkway toward his front door, wondering when the day would come that the alphabet boys jumped from bushes and hauled him to the Federal Detention Center in downtown Philadelphia.

Inside his home, Lex tossed a shopping bag onto an olive-green mohair love seat and yelled for his fiancé,

Desiree. He smelled fried chicken, the only meat that she didn't burn up, while mentally planning to microwave a frozen pizza. He kicked off his wing tips and picked through the mail. He had a letter from his mother, who had been locked down before he was born. Walking to the kitchen he read the letter.

Dear Alexis,

As usual, I am fine, and checking in on my baby, well man. I enjoyed our visit last weekend and am sad that you couldn't come for Christmas. Guess, I gotta realize, well, I have, that you're developing your own family. When that wench (lol) gonna have me a grand baby. I got another $1,000 on my account from you, and I sent it to my Bank of America account, as usual. I am going to email you later. Just wanted to drop you a personal letter. Don't forget to contact my lawyer.

Love,

Mom

Lex folded the letter and pulled out his cell phone. He began to type an E-mail to his mother and thought, *the feds let inmates send out emails, what's next?* He thanked her for the letter and promised to get her an appeals lawyer.

Desiree was at the kitchen table, telephone cradled between her shoulder and ear, as she flipped through a magazine. Lex leaned down to kiss her, and she pulled her head away. *Why do I put up with this bitch anymore,* Lex thought and pulled a box of pizza from the freezer. He had intentions to aggravate her to the point that she would go to her home, or force him to storm out, pretending to be angry.

"I know you see me frying chicken?"

"Indeed." *That's 'bout all you fry.*

To the person on the phone, Desiree said, "Let me call you back, girl. This nut putting a pizza in the microwave as if I am not in here slavin' like Aunt Jemima for his ass." She slammed the phone onto the marble island and jumped into Lex's face. He smelled her fragrances; many of them he had bought. He stared hard into her golden eyes and admired her full pinkish lips, an asset that he adored.

"Why the fuck did you leave me in the house all night by my damn self?" she asked, opening the microwave door. She then tossed the pizza onto the floor. "You didn't fucking call or respond to my text." He just looked blankly at her. "Answer me, dammit."

Lex snapped out of his vision of him handcuffing her to a tree and driving 80-mph into her. He smiled, and said, "I was taking care of business. Bought you some Louboutin's and Blahnik's, too. They're in the car." He did not tell her that she was nothing more than a showpiece, and he kept her up-to-the-minute for his image, not hers. Desiree was a bad high-yellow woman with sexy strawberry freckles, but Lex's craft had redefined bad woman. Her having video vixen looks was no longer impressive to him.

"I'm sick and tired of you ripping and running the streets."

"Getting my money, too."

"While I sit the fuck in the house bored to death."

"You don't look dead to me." *Wish you were, though. Keep it up, and you may wind up dead.* Exiting the kitchen, he said, "I don't feel like hearing this, ma. What the hell am I supposed to do, take you on route with me?"

"No, and you need to stop stealing."

Lex ignored her stupidity. *And I don't steal, dumb ass. I con. Call me Mr. Confidence.* He sat on the sofa and turned on the 3D projector that displayed the Maxwell *Pretty Wings* video, and he wished that she would fly away.

"You're not paying me any fuckin' attention."

"Naw," he said and added a condescending sneer that she watched him give men that he saw beneath him.

"You think that everything is a joke."

"Not everything, just you."

"I hate your arrogant ass."

"Need a ride home?"

Desiree mushed Lex's head. Lex jumped to his feet and she jumped back. He got deep into her face.

"That was your only time. And I don't give a fuck about anyone in your family, Des."

All that remained was good sex. No matter the time or place, if his penis was hard, she softened it. If her pussy was moist, he wet it. Lex had grown up, life was more than sex, and he had had enough of Desiree Garner.

She screamed at the top of her lungs, lunged forward slapping his face and upper body uncontrollably. Instinctively, and having built a wealthy coffer of anger, Lex slung her like a lawn chair in a hurricane. She blew into the dining room and grabbed the table cover in a bad attempt to break her fall. Lex watched an exorbitant eight-piece dinnerware set crash to the polished hardwood floor. The dishes broke along with a Swarovski case that contained fresh crocuses. Desiree sprang to her feet and rushed toward Lex. She leaped toward him like a lion attacking its prey. He sidestepped and she slammed into the hardwood. Before she stood, he jumped onto her and pinned her to the floor with his dick in her face. He could turn this into a sexual moment or use it to solidify their breakup. He had needed a great reason to kick her to the curb and her violent episode qualified as one.

"Lex, you're hurting me," she yelled while wiggling to become free. "I'm going to get a splinter on my ass, boy. Get off me."

"Stop squirming and what I tell you about calling me a boy?"

She spat and her DNA landed on his shoulder.

"Des, you tried to spit in my face. Are you serious?" he asked, pressing down on her. "I should hawk spit right into your eye." He stared at her menacingly.

"Fuck you." She then screamed, "Rape. Help me. Get off me, Alexis Burton." She prayed that the neighbors had heard her.

This bitch is trying to get me booked, Lex thought. Then came a knock at the front door.

11

For a Friday and his second day home, life could not have been more serene. Don Juan parked the Range Rover along the Happy Hollow Playground basketball courts, his childhood stomping ground. He was a summer B-ball league champion and a boxer on the recreation center's team. He was 14-1 before he decided that he had a more promising career as a dope dealer. His six years in the pen, helped him miss a major drug raid that sent his boys to federal jails or witness protection in Montana. On the flip side, he had just shopped until he could not carry another bag. He had taken a shower, gotten dressed, and hopped out the Range and peeked at a Harry Winston platinum watch.

It was midnight. He strolled across Wayne Avenue and slid into Charlie B's Bar.

In the vestibule, Hank, the bouncer, was shocked to see Don Juan. He didn't show it, though. He frisked Don Juan, ignoring his pistol, and Don Juan pushed open the door as T-Pain's *I'm Sprung* blasted through the system. Before the door shut behind him the music screeched to a halt. DJ Lisa Love was on the ones and twos.

"Y'all bitches better give it up. Look who done bust down the prison gates. Don-fuckin-Juan. They told me this boss was out. Bartender, all his bottles are on me tonight." Don Juan had on iced out Roberto Cavalli shades on his face, which sparked DJ Lisa to say, "Let me play *Flashin' Lights* for this flashy guy."

Don Juan grabbed a seat at the end of the bar, nearest to the door. His unofficial seat. *I'm fucking back,* he thought as the barmaid slid a blood orange drink in front of him.

"Not that you need it after jail, but two of these will keep your dick hard a week," the barmaid told him, and then dropped a straw in his drink.

"What is it?" he asked and took a big sip without the straw.

"X-rated Fusion liqueur, rum, grenadine, and a blood orange slice. I'm Dawn, by the way."

Don Juan looked over at the small dance floor in the corner and watched couples grinding hard.

Woman begging to be hammered.

Men looking to pound.

Hotel plans being made.

Over at a row of booths, business meetings took place. Some men were at the pool table playing with a woman whose skirt was so short that each time she bent over her thong showed. Don Juan was sure that she was hustling the men out of their money on the table, and she'd get one or two of them in the bedroom later, as well.

Very conspicuously, Popz strolled over to Don Juan and introduced himself. He shook Don Juan's hand and slipped him a small piece of paper. Popz was a light brown skinned man with a rugged look and a complimentary crooked tooth. He had a bald head that shinned each time the strobe light hit his head. He told Don Juan, "I know you're about your work. Get at me when you ready to get it poppin'. My dad, Big Sam, told me to look out for you."

"No doubt," Don Juan said and slipped the number in his pocket. He nodded to Popz and he walked away.

Don Juan sipped the drink and wondered which woman he'd be taking to a hotel that night. He wasn't taking anyone to his crib. He feared they'd rob him or set him up. Suddenly, things spun in slow motion and it wasn't the drink.

* * *

Sherry's man dipped into the bar with her trailing behind him. She was an attractive woman. Her hair was tight with her breasts pushing out a tight shirt. Jeans painted on. He remembered that time that he had measured Sherry's waist. It was 23 inches and she had a 36-inch ass, too. He watched her drape her arm around her lame man.

Where the fuck is my daughter? This bitch is out here with this clown. Don Juan was pissed that he had put a stolen cop gun in his face. *I got to get the drop on him ASAP.*

Don Juan was tapped on his shoulder. He turned and saw an attractive, exclusive looking woman who took his mind off Sherry and Bozo.

Boldly, she said, "Lemme holla at you fam'."

"Talk dirty to me, ma," he said and followed her scent towards the booths.

Settled into a booth, the woman sent the barmaid to fetch a bottle of champagne. When the woman stepped off, Don Juan's new friend said, "Can I be honest with you?"

"I wouldn't want it any other way," Don Juan replied staring at her intensively. He mastered how to attract a woman with his sex appeal. "Can I ask you a question?" He certainly wanted to know why she picked him.

"I've been waiting for your return."

"I don't know you."

She leaned over the table, looked deep into his eyes, and said, "I know you. Don Juan Jackson, 28, big ole dick." She leaned back and said, "Now, you may ask you a question?"

"I got a room at the Holiday Inn. You spending the night with me?"

"Of course. We gon' sip this bottle. Let all these bitches wish that they were me, and then in a half, we can be out."

"What's your name?"

"Theory."

12

A ringing telephone could brag about ruining a mood.

Don Juan sat in the back seat of his Range Rover, polishing off a weed-filled blunt, ignoring his cell phone. He was parked outside a row of rooms at the Holiday Inn. Theory was in the hourly motel room stripping at Don Juan's request. He had wanted his night to be worth it. Mr. Confidence had her right where he wanted her, drunk and lusting for him. Prior to sending her into a cheap motel room to undress, he had let her fondle his chiseled physique under the condition that she let him rub all over her, too. How could she refuse his hands roaming about her soft body? That's what she wanted, and he planned to give it to her.

Don Juan saw the motel light flash on and then off. His cue. Showtime. He lowered the truck's radio before killing the engine. The room door swung open and a work of art stood in the doorway. A very vanilla, Theory stood there with her nipples hardened and at full attention. Full D-cups hung in the air. Freshly shaved middle exposed. A fat ass peeked from behind her slim waist and thighs.

Don Juan broke his neck to get out the car, but his cell phone rang. He looked at the phone's screen. *What the fuck you need, Lex? Not right now buddy.* He pressed IGNORE and slammed the truck door shut behind him. He pulled his T-shirt over his head and let Theory see how his hard work in the pen had paid off. She admired a Philadelphia skyline tattoo emblazoned all over his back. He winked his chest at her, and she smiled. *I'mma beat that shit up,* he thought as his cell phone rang again, and he unbuttoned his pants. He locked the hotel room door, kicked his sneakers into a corner, and then snatched his jeans off. A song by Keisha Coles and Monica played in the background on the hotel room's alarm clock. He licked his lips at Theory and slipped off his boxers. His disco stick came out; and, once again his cell phone rang. He glanced at the floor where his cell was and then at Theory, deciding which one was more important.

Theory was stretched across a full-sized bed, her legs spread apart, with the heels of her feet hanging off the edges of the bed. Theory won the war between her with the phone when she tightened her pussy lips and made them blow a kiss at him. Don Juan crawled between her legs and kissed her inner thighs. He planted salacious kisses around her love box until his tongue found her treasure. He licked softly before he nibbled and pressed his tongue harder on her spot. She ran her fingers through Don Juan's short wavy hair and massaged his head and shoulders. His big hands explored her breasts, as he feasted on her middle. He felt her quivering and snatched his face from between her legs; he wanted her to come around his dick.

He kissed up her stomach, circling his tongue around her belly button, and then her nipples. When his tongue reached her earlobe, he plunged his dick inside her. A few deep strokes and she came; her muscles tightening fiercely around his tool. He loved that feeling. Her juices soaked his dick and stomach as he pounded in and out of her. She wrapped her legs around his waist, grabbed his ass, and pulled him deeper into her. She gyrated her hips musically.

He liked that.

A lot.

And then he came.

His cell phone rang.

Don Juan kept pounding as he snatched up the phone. "Lex, you better be dying."

"Worse. I'm at the 15th police district. Come get me out before they take me to the county. I am not trying to see CFCF."

13

Alexis Burton once had a large circle in his criminal life, but that crowd had ruined his chance to avoid prison. Some of them were lazy and only around for the benefits associated with being the groupie of a con man. It hadn't taken him long to surmise that they were really an entourage. Don Juan, however, was different. Lex strolled out the precinct and hopped in Don Juan's Range Rover. No one spoke because silence was essential for the moment. Thoughts had to be collected.

Don Juan was a street hustler, yet he understood the world Lex had been turned on to. The white man's world. Both men were Virgo's; but, their very different backgrounds was the foundation of their friendship. By comparison, though, they were both grimy go-getters that went about getting a dollar differently, until a day ago. Their teaming up was genius. Why not? Their street-smarts and book-smarts were the perfect tandem.

Many took Don Juan as a pretty boy without brains, that masculine representation of the dumb blonde; but, he had a street swagger that was perfect to participate in Lex's white-collar wizardry. It was unfortunate for bankers that, despite Lex being in the white-collar life and Don Juan in the streets, both of their worlds revolved around money. And they planned to get plenty of it, avoiding coffin nails and guilty verdicts along the way.

Lex laid back in the leather seat and listened to Young Jeezy. The way Lex saw things, he was doomed to hit the criminal path from the jump; after all, he was born in a county jail. The only good to evolve from the situation was, he was given to a loving white couple and raised in a stable high-income home. One thing was certain, though, he was not white and could not avoid a trip to the 15th district.

When Don Juan reached Cottman Avenue and Roosevelt Boulevard, he flipped a right then headed in the direction of Lex's crib.

"What happened, dawg?"

"Desiree pressed charges on me."

"What? For what?"

"Same shit like Sherry did to you. Nothing."

"Word." Don Juan didn't know what that meant exactly, but it was not the time to press the issue.

"Don't take me home. Drop me up Chestnut Hill."

"What about your car?"

"I'll get a cab home. I gotta do something, I should have been done."

"Dawg, you gotta kill that bitch next year," Don Juan said and laughed. "If you kill her now, the cops are coming straight at you."

"I can kill that bitch right now, man. But I ain't doing that. I got a crazy gig for us in the a.m. by the way, just drop me off for now."

14

A knockout beauty opened the front door of a stately Chestnut Hill home. A silk robe posed as the second layer of skin on her luscious body. Lex suavely leaned on the entryway of the home with hopelessness spread across his face. Ijanay looked at him puzzled because he had never been to her home. She didn't even know how he had found her place. She batted her bright brown eyes and furrowed her eyebrows at him in an attempt to stall her response to his bold visit. A few days earlier, Lex had warned her that actions spoke louder than words.

With unintentional seduction, Ijanay ran her fingers through her bottled-auburn hair, and asked, "What are you doing here?"

"I broke up with her," he replied and flashed her the engagement ring that he had given the woman that had him arrested. He tossed it into the night.

Ijanay, at first, looked at him confused, then she leaned on him.

For seven months they had known each other. She had escorted her 8th grade class of students to the Philadelphia Museum of Art. In the Egyptian section, Lex spoke to her. They chatted about the so-called step pyramid at Saqqarah, the earliest known pyramid. Lex had impressed her, however, she refused to pass along her number at the museum in the presence of her class. A week later, he had sent four dozen roses to Clarence E. Pickett Middle School, with a card inviting her to Nubian's, an Egyptian themed restaurant. Despite their uncharacteristic pull toward one another, they are friends, he had a fiancé, and she had a secret that was not his business.

"So what does that mean?" she asked.

He grabbed her waist and pulled her closer to him. Her back rested against his chest snuggly. "Can we go inside, Ijanay? I'm hungry and tired."

Ijanay wasn't a woman typically lost for words, but at that time she was tight-lipped. She spun around and looked at him deeply into his eyes. There was something different about him. "It's three in the morning. Have you been up all night?" she asked, resting her arms on his shoulders.

He hugged her tightly, and whispered, "She had me locked up."

"You gotta be kidding me. For what?" she asked, leaning back from him. Ijanay liked his quiet, but direct aura. He wasn't spineless. He wasn't a thug. But he was right in the middle of the two; strong enough to like art and knew when to send flowers. "Come on. Let's get off this porch."

She stepped into her colonial home and locked the door behind them. Everything was neat and inspired by Art History. A coffee table full of news periodicals. Red brick walls were covered in paintings. Sculptures strategically placed. The home of a smart woman. Just what had known she was. She was 36 years-old, attractive, and had a beautiful mind. He liked those things. He was even more into the fact that she would not entertain another woman's man. He was hopeful that that picture would change, as she led him to the kitchen.

Lex followed her derriere along the way, as he told her about his drama with Desiree. Ijanay was shocked and unimpressed, but she was smart enough to know that there were two sides to every story. Despite her pure chocolate complexion, Ijanay blushed for no reason other than being in Lex's company. She listened to him while cooking eggs scrambled with cheese, onions and tomatoes, turkey sausage links, and two Belgian waffles topped with strawberries and powdered sugar.

He ate and sipped a heavily champagne laced mimosa. He admired the beautiful flow of Ijanay's movement around the state-of-the-art kitchen. He knew she was a tidy woman because she dressed finely and neatly, but her kitchen was spotless. None of her tweed suits compared to the robe that he wanted her to take off. He needed something to get his mind off Desiree and that nonsense.

After he had eaten, Ijanay collected his plate, glass and placed them in a dishwasher. When she turned around, Lex was on her.

"You scared me, boy," she said and playfully pushed him, allowing her hands to rest on his broad chest.

"Man. I am a man, sweetheart," he said correcting her. "And you don't have to be scared of me. To you, I am harmless."

"I'm not scared of you. I'm just not used to a man being behind me in my kitchen."

He pulled the rope on her robe and her breasts shot out.

POW!

"Not used to anyone admiring your priceless body in your kitchen, either, huh?" he asked, pulling her into his arms. He pressed his erection against her and leaned in to kiss her when he saw a shadow towering over them. *What the fuck?* Lex whipped around defensively.

"Mommie," said Ijanay's four-year-old secret, Payton.

15

Saturday morning, Don Juan posing as Anwar Muhammad was the first man on the Jaguar showroom floor. He enjoyed a glass of Dom Perignon Rose 1996, as Matthew Nixon showed him the colors the car he planned to steal was offered in. The men developed a buyer-seller relationship, the moment a tuxedo-clad driver let Don Juan out of a limousine in front the Jaguar dealership. Matthew had greeted Don Juan on the curb. He loved that Don Juan vowed to drive from the dealership and had sent his driver home.

For a half-hour, the men perused and test drove different models, before Don Juan settled on the Jaguar XJ8. He had participated in the car buying experience, pretending that he had to decide on the perfect color; however, the chop shop that he planned to sell the XJ8 wanted a metallic gold exterior with cream-colored insides. Don Juan planned to buy the vehicle with his weapon of mass destruction: an ink pen.

"Gold is a neat color," Matthew said, after Don Juan's selection. He slid the binder of colors into a credenza and then told Don Juan, "I still think you're rather young for the XJ8."

"Matthew, I am the newest executive at the largest law firm in the city. I need this kind of car. Clients require this. Certainly, an XJ8 compliments my three-million dollar a year salary," Don Juan said, lying. He sat back and sipped his champagne. He then pulled his identification from a wallet and passed it to a car salesman. "Besides, I'm not as young as I look." He sat up and whispered, "And no one needs to know that. You know what I mean."

"Certainly, Mr. Muhammad..."

"Anwar."

"Thirty-five, though. I'm impressed. I didn't have you a day over 24."

"No one does," Don Juan said, as the phone on the desk rang.

"Excuse me," Matthew said, taking the call.

The caller said, "Mr. Nixon, this is FBI Agent Richard Davidson. Withhold your surprise, if any. The man in your office is a fraud. I do not know what name or stolen identity that he has used, but I assure you that it's not his own. Let me get an OK, Mr. Nixon."

"OK..."

"Wouldn't want to awake the dead to this investigation. I assure you, whatever credentials that he has given you are counterfeit, albeit they will pass your credit approval process. I need him to leave your dealership behind the wheel of whatever he wants. Got that?"

"Uh...I don't know. I better..."

"You better stop right there. The Bureau's two-year investigation hinges on this bust. I gotta catch that madman red-handed. Pay very close attention to everything he touches in your office. A team is in place, milling about the dealership prepared to dust for prints. I need you to fax a copy of any documents that he signs to...grab a pen, 215-555-4126...to me Agent Davidson.

"Lower Merion PD is set up to greet him before he leaves Montgomery County and crosses into Philadelphia. They'll stall him while I verify the stolen identity and stolen check or credit card he uses so that we can get that guy off the streets. Now, what's it going to be, Mr. Nixon?"

Matthew thought a moment before, he said, "I have your number. I'll get those documents to you as soon as I finish with this client. In the meantime, I have to be going."

"Good man, Mr. Nixon."

Matthew Nixon hung up the phone, and said to Don Juan, "Now where were we?"

"You were putting me behind the wheel of my well-deserved Jaguar."

"Yeah! You've earned it." *You're so busted, pal.*

16

It was not the first time that he drove behind the wheel of a vehicle with seats that automatically adjusted the height of the driver. Don Juan drove across City Avenue —out of Montogomery County and into Philadelphia County—in a purloined $90,000 Jaguar XJ8. He was without a care in the world. He had played the car salesman and made a successful getaway, leaving behind a counterfeit check valued at $18,679.23 for a down payment.

In West Philadelphia, he pulled into a gas station and disembarked the vehicle. He was met by Lex—the chauffeur—that had dropped him at the dealership. Lex hopped out a tow truck. He had lost the tuxedo and wore a dirty jumper. He tossed Don Juan a car cover and a black Dickey set.

Don Juan covered the vehicle as Lex connected the Jaguar to the tow truck. The Jag disappeared and Don Juan slipped out of his costume and into a Dickey set and work boots. With the car covered and safely secured to the tow truck, both men hopped into the truck and Lex drove down the county dividing City Avenue towards I-76.

"How long do you think Matthew Nixon will wait for the FBI?"

"Don't know," Lex said, smiling. "I do know that before he hung up with me, he was anxious to bust you. Here's the fax," he said, laughing. "By the way, you're acting more and more like Mr. Anwar Muhammad."

17

Lex cruised in his BMW with Don Juan sprawled across the passenger seat He chuckled maniacally at the Jaguar dealerships expense. Lex was impressed with Don Juan's adroitness. He watched his friend's chest rise and fall rapidly, a sure sign that he was glad he made an easy $30,000 from the theft. And it didn't involve a possible trip to the penitentiary for 30 years.

"You're not even close to getting the money," Lex said and turned rapper Jeezy up louder. His cell phone vibrated on his hip, and he checked the caller ID. *I don't feel like dealing with this bitch,* he thought. He had had a long night, an early morning, and no desire to be bothered by Desiree. She had messed up and he had a life to live. His magic show would go on. Knowing that prompted him to answer the phone to get under her skin.

"What's good?" Lex asked blithely into the phone, as if, he didn't have a concern in the world.

"Lex, I'm so sorry. I don't know what I was thinking."

"You wasn't, but don't trip. You're good."

"Why you acting like you don't care about me?" Desiree asked, seeming as if she was weeping. "I can't do this anymore, Lex. You gotta change how you be snapping at me when I only try to flirt with you to make you happy."

"You gon' have a hard life without me, Desiree. 'Cause I ain't changing anything."

"Lex, stop being so cold to me. You're mean to me all the time for no reason."

"That's funny. You had me booked, but you call me mean. Let's just let it burn."

"So, that's what you want?" she asked. He could hear the venom in her loaded question.

"The moment that I paid bail I wanted that."

"You know what? Fuck you," she said, laughing. "Ain't nobody really crying. I hate you. That's why I took $10,000 from you for being out all night. My life won't be nearly as hard as you thought it'd be. Tootles." She hung up.

Lex tossed his cell phone on the dashboard, and said, "I'm really going to kill that bitch. She stole that money that I had left over from New York."

"She's feeling herself, I see. Got you arrested. Stole from you. Why you going through this bullshit anyway?"

"I don't even know. I have outgrown her. She wasn't moving with me. I tried to give her all that I had. Besides, I learned a lesson from all this bullshit. I ain't never getting involved with two women like you did. I'm not like that. She's just always on some small minded shit and it aggravates me."

"You can't compare me to you. I had them both pregnant."

"My point exactly. Never will I do that. And I never have raw sex. A bitch ain't giving me shit and I don't want any accidents."

"You're too disciplined. And you sound crazy. You sound stuck up, saying you out grew your first love."

"Man, all she does is complain and shop. She's not on my level. She wanna be Taraji Henson in Baby Boy, but I want a woman like Gabrielle Union in Daddy's Little Girl."

"So, you're too good for a ghetto bitch, now?"

"What? All they're worried about is who got weed to smoke, something to drink, and welfare. I don't need a woman like that, man. And if all she has going on is a cashier job and The Dollar Store and no other aspirations, I am not interested."

"You sound like a white boy. Like you forgot where you came from."

"I didn't forget. I know what's out there and where I am going."

"You act like you had things rough in life."

"Man, you don't know anything. You met me in high school. Matter-of-fact, what you 'bout to do?"

"Nothing."

"Let me show you something."

18

Princeton, New Jersey was a small town, very attractive, and home to the Ivy League Princeton University. Lex drove along traditional Princeton Junction, passing quaint local shops and big retailers. The air was pine tree fresh. After getting off the junction, Lex maneuvered through small, tree-lined streets, passing by large wealthy homes.

"Mulberry Street? Where the hell you got me?"

"My parent's home."

Lex parked his BMW in a rotund driveway behind a Mercedes Benz E-350. There was a fountain in the middle of the driveway that sprayed a dazzling water show. A long balcony lined the front of the mini-manse, which covered a long porch. Sculptures of Greek gods and goddesses stood at the tops of the columns. A woman sat in expensive porch furniture reading. She was nicely dressed, slim, and donned over-sized shades with her hair pulled into a chignon.

"Who's the white lady?"

"My mom," Lex replied, hopping out of the car.

"Come on with the bullshit," Don Juan said and joined Lex as he walked toward the porch.

Lex hugged his mother and kissed her two cheeks. "How are you, mom?"

"Just fine. Would be much better if you called more often, though. Who's your friend?" Lex introduced them, and then she said, "Don Juan? Your mother gave you that name, or is that a street name?"

"It's my birth name, ma'am," Don Juan replied, smiling. He held out his hand to shake.

"Well, it's great to meet you, Don Juan," she said and smirked. "I was just editing this article before publication in the law journal."

"My mom is a professor of law at the University of Penn, but is also an adjunct professor at Princeton U," Lex told Don Juan. To his mother, he said, "We're going to the pool to chill out a bit. Needed to get out the city."

"I keep the pool filled just for you. Gretchen prepared coq au vin for lunch."

"Gretchen?" Don Juan whispered as they entered the home.

"The cook, Don Juan. The maid is Sarah. The butler is John. He is mom's driver, too, when she needs to get around."

* * *

The pool was shaped like a tear drop. Both men sat pool side in lounge chairs with cocktails that had umbrellas sticking out. Lex was smart and accounted for everything. Trust meant the world to him and his trust in Don Juan directed him to allow him into that world. Lex had Don Juan at his mother's pool where they could talk without interruption. Don Juan had been stripped of his clothing, and wore swimming trunks and a cotton monogram logo towel. Lex had clandestinely eliminated any doubt that their conversation was being recorded. Lex trusted Don Juan, but had grown up raised by a man drafted into the Waffen Schutzstaffel, prior to the man escaping to

America. Lex had been treated to rugged espionage tales not found in classic Tom Clancy novels.

After ten minutes of enjoying the warm breeze, Don Juan broke the silence. "How you got a white mom. Your dad must be..."

"Dead."

"Damn, my bad, bro."

"To hell with him. He was an Army man who beat my mother until she killed his ass. She's been in federal jail since before I was born. She gave birth to me in jail, and the Geiser's adopted me. My mom was the caretaker of their cerebral palsy child. Ms. Geiser's husband was deported, though. And that's when my mom's aunt Darlene went to court and took me from the Geiser's. She moved me Uptown to where I met you. And took me from this, thrusting me into the ghetto."

"Damn, I ain't even know that you were adopted, man. Why dude get deported?" Don Juan was curious, and deep into Lex's story. If he hadn't known how strong Lex was he would have felt sorry for him, even though, Don Juan had very few empathetic bones in his body.

"I can't believe that I am telling you all this," Lex said and sipped his cocktail. "Geiser, before he worked in Germany and Austria, was drafted into the Death's Head Battalion, an elite guard of the Nazi party. He guarded the perimeter of a concentration camp. In 1956, he came to America and worked as an engineer for the auto industry until German competitors, or Mercedes Benz, anonymously alerted the feds that he assisted in persecuting Jews. His citizenship was revoked in 1994 and he died before he could get the court to overturn the ruling to deport him. He's the one that taught me the con game that I am showing you now. He was the best."

Don Juan was lost for words. He was like a shy kid forced to read out loud. He had his own problems, but he listened as Lex spoke about his childhood, and that changed the game. Don Juan abused weed by 10, sold crack by 13, and had run away from home by 15. That was rough and an excuse for him to become loyal to the streets. Having dodged bullets and drug conspiracies clouded Don Juan into a belief that he had an upbringing harder than Lex. But, how so? Don Juan was not adopted because his mother killed his father. Don Juan knew that Lex's aunt was poor and they had run an extension cord from the neighbor's house to operate the refrigerator. Lex was teased for being dirty and wearing his cousin's clothing. Sitting poolside, sipping on vodka, Don Juan had no real idea as to who had it worse. Above all, Don Juan was a pretty boy, and so was Lex. Beneath that, though, they were different. The yin and the yang.

After a moment of taking in the conversation and another sip, Don Juan blurted, "I gotta get my daughter at six, bro."

"Aiight, cool. Take the rest of the day off. Tomorrow, too. You deserve it."

"You're a funny, dude. I don't work for you."

"I know. You work for yourself. Let's get out of here," Lex said, smiling. He stood, and said, "Before we roll, how much you wanna stack before you out the game?"

"Damn good question." Don Juan thought for a second. He didn't want to suggest too much and cause Lex to perceive him as greedy, but he didn't want to low ball and be deemed an underachiever. "Three mill," he said and then dove into the pool. He wanted to give Lex a chance to conjure up a reply.

"That's a great number," Lex said when Don Juan rose for air. "Just think about what you're going to do with the money to legalize it because that's going to be easy to get."

19

For ten minutes, Don Juan sat patiently outside Sherry's house. He couldn't wait for Trinity to come out. There was no doubt that Sherry was purposefully trying his patience. Had she known how prison had taught him to hurry up and wait, she would've had his child ready.

The front door opened and first out was Trinity, followed by Sherry, and then Rob. Trinity was dressed warmly, but her big hazel eyes, just like her daddy's, shone brightly in the sun. In true diva fashion, she slipped on pink shades and walked nonchalantly toward the curb. At that point, Don Juan stepped out of the truck and strolled onto the pavement.

"Daddy. Daddy. Daddy. Daddy," Trinity yelled and raced towards her father. Don Juan squatted down and she threw her arms around his neck. He picked her up and swung her in the air.

Don Juan whispered to her. "I miss you so much, Baby Girl."

"I miss you too, Daddy," she replied and kissed his forehead.

"You ready to go?"

"Yup," she said, and he put her down. She had grown so much. Trinity was tall, pretty-dark complexion, and had shoulder length hair pulled into two ponytails.

Don Juan strapped his daughter into a toddler car seat and stared hard at Sherry. He hated her at that time. How could she keep his precious jewel from him while he was incarcerated? He remembered that while Sherry worked he had cared for and loved Trinity so much as an infant that she had grown very close to her father. Their bond was unbreakable. One day Don Juan was going to attempt full custody of his child. He was so ecstatic that Sherry and Rob watched Trinity enthusiastically ran towards him. *Take that*, he thought.

"Yo, let me talk to you real quick," Sherry yelled at Don Juan.

She bounced down the stairs; no doubt, her breasts moved uncontrollably and Don Juan thought that she was trying to entice him. *Rotten bitch*, he thought.

When she was on the curb, he asked, "You saw how she ran to me?"

"So." Defiant. "You're her father, she's supposed to love you."

"Good 'cause if you ever try to bother our father/ daughter relationship, or let that clown you call your man harm her, I promise that your mother will bury you. Your friend will be found in the Delaware River neatly packed in a suitcase."

"Fuck you, jerk," she said to his back.

Don Juan hopped into the truck and asked Trinity what she wanted to do. He had forgotten all about Sherry's drama. *Forget that loser.*

"I want to get my nails and feet done, dad."

"What?" he asked, pulling off. Her request had thrown him off. *What happened to play land at McDonald's or something like that?* He calmed down and thought that he could take her on a father/daughter day at the spa. The act would get him a much-needed massage and make him the best dad in the world. "Let's do it," he said.

"Yes," she said and pumped a fist into the air. "Daddy, I got a joke for you. I know a lot of jokes."

"OK, shoot." *Damn, I miss my baby*, he thought. *Look at her all smart and pretty. I made that.* Conceit.

20

That evening Lex was balls deep into a pretty little-med student. He had women all over the country, but he never had an intimate love affair on Desiree. Sure, he had sex, but nothing more. No dates. No long phone calls. He never attached himself to any women, and was very careful not to hurt her. He only desired to give her the best. He wasn't a disloyal man and he did love Desiree. But at the time, Taneesha was beneath him, legs rested on his shoulders, as he dangerously pounded in and out of her. Erotically, he assaulted her. Why? Because Desiree had stolen from him, and since he couldn't punish her, he murdered Taneesha. And she loved every stab.

Behind the glitz of Taneesha working as an intern at The University of Pennsylvania Hospital, she liked to have Lex play a doctor on her; giving her vaginal and oral exams. What Taneesha adored about Lex was his Superman-like transformation. He was calm and cool, respectful and rational; despite being an incorrigible thief. But when he stepped into the bedroom, that was like Clark Kent dashing into a telephone booth.

"You like when the dick doctor dicks you down?" he asked and pulled all but the head of his penis out of her.

"Yes, Doctor Lex." She moaned, winced, and smiled as he snaked his dick—long and wide as the Mississippi River back into her.

Desiree did not have any casual or direct proof that Lex had ever cheated on her, but she always accused him. He couldn't understand why would she creep into his home and rob him for $10,000. The thought of her having him arrested, and then returning to his domain kept him from coming because his mind was on that and not the sex. He surmised that that was a plus for Taneesha.

He simply wanted to relieve stress with Taneesha. He pretended to be an hour man, not a one-minute man. Why didn't Desiree understand that when he came home from a hard day, he did not want stress? He had had enough of that in the streets. Although he committed white collar crimes, lawmakers had heightened the ante, passing tougher fraud-related sentences.

Taneesha rattled and came a third time, as the home phone rang. Taneesha screamed so loudly that perhaps the neighbors checked to see if he and Desiree enjoyed make-up sex, or she faced death. He had never had another woman in his home.

"Don't answer it, Doctor."

The house phone stopped ringing.

His cell phone rang next.

Steadily he thrust faster and harder. The slapping sound of their bodies bellowed in the air. He checked the caller ID, and then answered the phone. The person on the other end was silent, no doubt, listening to the sounds of lovemaking. Without disconnecting the caller, Lex sat the phone on the nightstand. The med student was glad that, he had decided to give her his full attention.

"Come for me again, ma."

"Yes, Doctor."

Lex imagined Desiree on the other end of the phone going off. She had no idea that things had just begun. She had better move on while ahead.

21

A sprawling crammed city, Philadelphia had a dose of winter snow flurries and aggressive traffic. Despite that, Don Juan moseyed down Germantown Avenue, after he dropped his daughter at home. He had lifted a weight from his chest, having rehearsed his lines to say to his daughter for a year. With that over, he had something new to deal with.

Under the false quietness, Don Juan Jackson in a long sleeve button-up and dark jeans, just an ordinary thug, pulled into Philadelphia's notorious Puerto Rican section: The Bad Lands. Don Juan was there with a purpose. That derelict area of North Philadelphia was dirty and had cars with banging systems, neon lights and illegal tint. On an average day, the sidewalks were clogged with ten-year-olds that pushed dime bags of everything imaginable. Behind the scenes, though, tons of cocaine and heroin was distributed by the Latinos. They had a renowned reputation for shelling out a good product. And, Don Juan after six long years wanted parts of that trade. But first, he needed a woman to help him get in.

Don Juan parked, strolled down Lehigh Avenue, and dipped into Mommies. This was Don Juan's first trip to the strip club that hosted beautiful, young woman, but he had long ago planned this visit. Don Juan was impressed by the gentleman club's sophisticated ambiance. The club was in the hood, but the kind of space that Hugh Hefner hosted a wet T-shirt fiesta. On the stage was a petite Asian woman that had front and back enhancements. She worked her way out of a kimono and around a pole. Her allure seduced Don Juan, but he was on business.

Don Juan grabbed a Heineken bottle from the bar and slipped into a booth, where he sat and scoped out the whore-house. Certainly, the blowjob performed in the corner was not legal at a grander club, but cops frequented Mommies for good pussy, not arrests. Every man not at the stage, drowning Asia Doll in loot had two females on him. Mommies had a 3:1 woman to man ratio. The back room treatment was priced like the Bunny Ranch in Nevada.

Twenty minutes later, Asia Doll collected her money and left the stage. She made way for Taster's Choice, a coffee colored Panamanian woman that knew very little English, but she could have sex in every language that spanned the globe. She was done up in a soccer uniform, swaying her hips to R. Kelly's *Seems Like Your Ready*.

Continuing to scan the club, Don Juan noticed a victim. He thought of resorting to his robbery days, and that was stupid. But, hey, this man had something coming. The man appeared high off drugs, was flanked by hookers, and dressed in a cheap suit, as if he had power.

Maybe he did.

The man was tall, had broad masculine shoulders, and dimples when he smiled. He caught Don Juan plotting and traipsed through Mommies as if he owned it. Don Juan watched him glide across the room, and the sea of patrons moved out of his path. He squinted oddly at Don Juan, as he approached Don Juan's booth.

The man looked evil and then his mood shifted to a half-smile.

Over R. Kelly's smooth groove the man held out his hand and said, "What a coincidence?"

Don Juan stared at the man and ignored his hand. He simply furrowed his brow. His body language indicated that he did not want company. The man sat anyway; fucking Don Juan's baby mama wasn't enough.

22

"You're arrogant for a broke man fresh outta jail," Rob said, comically. He chuckled.

This fool got me fucked up. In one swift motion, Don Juan tugged the bottom of his shirt and highlighted the gun at his waist, before he grinned. "Don't have an accident up in this bitch."

"Come on. You know..."

"Man, I'm trying to scope the broads, get some head, and be out. I ain't got no rap for you." Don Juan sipped his beer. He was finished with Rob.

"Well then, let me get to the point."

"Spear me."

"Maybe I will. But I doubt it," Rob replied, his face twisted with horror. He pulled out his cell phone. "I have some photos to show you."

"I've seen her naked. I don't give a fuck about no pics. You should hope, I never get the urge to fuck her because I can, very easily."

"I wouldn't care, bruh. She's bait. Take a look at the photos."

Don Juan flipped through the photo gallery on the cell phone. One-by-one they chronicled his late three days. The limo ride. The first ride in the Range Rover. Leaving the soul food restaurant in New York City. Shopping at Bloomingdale's. Buying the Jaguar.

"They're not your best pics, but, hey, there are no professional photographers here. Let me be frank. It's you or Lex," Rob said and smiled. He opened his blazer and flashed a badge.

"You a cop?" A dumb question. "Why you want, Lex? He ain't got shit to do with our problem."

"We don't have a problem. Never did. Here's the deal, I know all about Lex. Not as slick as he thinks he is, but I want Popz more. Deliver him to me and you and Lex get a pass."

This dude thinks that I am a fool. Don Juan was a quick thinker. Rob, had pictures, so this was no joke. And Don Juan didn't treat it as one. He pulled a wad of money from his jeans pocket and slid it across to Rob. Rob was dressed in that cheap business suit, so Don Juan thought he was a cheap businessman.

Rob blinked at the audacity. The blinking seemed uncontrollable. Don Juan's eyes were glassy with confusion, studying the stranger. Rob gathered the bills and walked over to Taster's Choice. He told her to have a Happy Christmas and tossed Don Juan's $3,000 at her. Don Juan stared Rob down with a hard look that couldn't be cut with a dagger.

Back at the table, Rob asked, "You enjoyed your visit with Trinity."

"Keep my baby out of this, man, I swear..."

"You swear, what?" Rob said and leaned across the booth's table. "She told me that you bought her a lot of things. But all I want is Popz. Or, I promise you'll never live to buy your daughter anything again. Got that?"

"Fuck you."

"Naw, I am not that way, gay boy. I do the fucking, and by the looks of things, you're being fucked raw."

Rob stood. "I'll use lube if you do what you're supposed to do for me. But I'll fuck you long and hard without grease if I do not get what I want."

23

For Monday morning's caper, the thorough con man wore his standard costume of highly exorbitant designer labels. That day he donned Gucci wingtips and carried a briefcase. Approached by a Baltimore, Maryland banker, he cracked a sly smile. That day, he was Karlton Dawson, and he had a corporate check that purported to be genuine, that he would deposit and cash. He planned to accomplish both, without tipping anyone that he was really born Alexis Burton, and he was a complete fraud.

Customers zipped around the bank and the employees went about their daily routines. Lex masqueraded around in a full red beard strapped to his flawless skin, and his hair was dyed burnt-red. He had an expensive makeup artist sprinkle freckles strategically around his face. Lex wore the makeup with great pride; and as funny as it sounded, he proved the ultimate purpose for male makeup: stealing.

Karlton Dawson sat behind a cheap desk in a Wachovia Bank branch. He cleared his throat, prepared to use his polished graduate student voice, and Steven Spielberg yelled action. The banker, who was more suited to win America's Next Top Model, asked how could she help him, and with grand dignity, he began the show.

"I've had an unfortunate loss, ya see. My father was killed tragically, and I inherited a rather large sum of money. All of which is governed by a trust fund banker, whose more like a cop protecting *my* money. Except for this," he said, opening his briefcase, "check. I've been saving cash and bought this to store in a safe deposit box, but I fear that the trust fund cop will snoop around and find it. Can you help me hide $325,000.00?"

The banker pulled at her ear and then smiled. "I'm sure we can," she said, batting her eyelashes. She snatched up the check and looked it over. "And this is drawn on our bank, Mr. Dawson, so we can have immediate access to the money. Do you have an account with us?"

"No."

"Shame on you," she said, smiling.

"I know. That's why I really need you, Ms. Tanner." He needed her more than she imagined he'd bet.

"Well, we have a fine depository system, and we can hide anything."

You can hide this dick in ya mouth, too, he thought, but he said, "For a fee, I bet."

"Touché." She tapped a few keys on her keyboard, and then said, "I just emailed our Security VP. I think I need special clearance to proffer you an alias package like we do the celebrities."

"Really," he said, relaxing in his chair. "Sounds interesting. Tell me about that package."

"We legally help customers invest their funds without guys like Forbes or the IRS knowing unless you report it. We can make 325K do somersaults and triple, Mr. Dawson, and only you'd know."

"That's even better than I planned. Call me, Karl. That's what my friends call me."

* * *

Lex walked out of the bank into a late December ray of sun, further reddening his facial beard. Park Avenue was flooded with pedestrians, despite that, though, he peeled off his beard. *Much better. It was hot in that bank.* He continued toward the Baltimore Penn Station, just another cocky, nicely dressed man headed from Baltimore to Philadelphia. Only he was clearly distinguishable. A banker had convinced him that he was going to need to hire a Wall Street accounting firm to do his taxes. That was so unnecessary because as soon as he had online access to the account, he planned to wire the money to Japan.

And then to Russia.

Next to Iraq.

Before it landed safely in the Cayman Islands.

American authorities would lose their breath trying to track the bank's money.

Like a seasoned Secret Service Agent, Lex slipped an earpiece into his ear and called, Ijanay. After three rings, she answered and announced that she was at the school.

"But you're on recess, right, Ms. Hyde."

"I am, but that's 42-minutes that I have to get work done. Besides that, I don't take personal calls at school, Mr. Alexis Burton."

"Thanks for taking this one." He loved the way she said his name.

"Well, the last time we met you were fresh out of jail. I was hoping this wasn't an emergency."

"A little it is," he said. "I'm still in New York, but I plan to head home early." He hated to lie to her, but that trait was the key to his DNA makeup. "I need an emergency date at a fine restaurant. I'll pay for your babysitter."

"My mother, but..."

"Come on, Ijanay, please. I know what you're thinking, but I'm done with her, trust me. I have been a while now. I was honest when I told you 'bout my relationship wit' her. And in my defense, while with her I never made a sexual advance towards you. I've been emotionally done with her for some time. I've mentally moved on. All I'm asking for is a dinner date. When was the last time you've been on one?"

"It's been some time, but what kind of example would I be for Payton if I go out on a school night."

"Ijanay are you serious?"

"Yes, I am very selective about what she's exposed to."

"One night. I have to see you. It's an emergency."

"I don't know."

"Of course you do. Whatever happened in your past, let it go."

"Lex, you have no clue about my past, but it plays a pivotal role in my discipline."

"Let's have dinner and you can tell me all about it."

"Maybe, I don't want that."

"Come on, it'll be fun."

"You're so charming. That's scary."

"I work on Wall Street, so I charm to eat," he said and chuckled. "This is the real me that you're getting, though."

"Tell you what, let's do an in-house dinner at my home?"

"Deal. What time? What are you cooking?

"Eight. Soul food."

24

Don Juan strolled around the Philadelphia downtown Gallery Mall. He was simply passing time and thinking about the 9,000-ways to kill Rob. He walked passed Horizon Books, a black-owned bookstore, and saw an author doing a book signing. He remembered being arrested with the man peddling his books and decided to stop and check him up.

He approached the man, and said, "I see you made it out and got your book poppin'." He picked up the man's book. It was titled, The Take by L. Brown.

"Yeah, man," L said while he autographed a young lady's book. He took a picture with her and then she walked away. "How long you been out?"

"A few months," Don Juan said, reading the synopsis of the book. "This book talks about real Uptown spots?"

"Yeah, that's some good shit, too."

"Bet, I'mma cop this jawn."

Don Juan paid for the book and had L sign it. They took a pic and Don Juan said, "I'mma post this on IG and FB and get some hoes down here to cop." His cell phone rang. "I gotta take this call. Get money, my dude."

In the phone's receiver, Don Juan heard Lex. "What's good man? I am on the train back from B-more."

"Ain't shit. We gotta rap, though, face to face. We have a serious problem."

"We do," Lex said and smiled. "I don't have any problems."

"Man, my BM's boyfriend is on some crazy shit."

"You better handle that fool then. I am not getting into that."

"You will when you hear this shit, homie. I am downtown, so I will meet you at the train station to tell you all about this shit."

25

Lex pulled up into a parking space on Ijanay's block and smiled. He was finally on an official date with a woman that was modest, had class, and self-respect. He opened up his glove compartment and sprayed one shot of Romeo Gigli cologne onto his collar. He was prepping for the grand hug that he planned to get from Ijanay. He wanted to bring the scent of a strong man into her home. He wanted to let it linger after he left.

When Lex got out of the car, he looked at himself from head to toe and smiled. *You a bad mutha fucka now go get ya woman,* he thought and walked to the door of Ijanay's home. He rang the bell and patiently waited.

Ijanay opened the door wearing jeans, a button-up, and pumps. Lex admired her simple look and found it interesting that she wasn't dressed over the top. It was special to him that she was a simple, modest woman that he prayed could handle him lavishing her with gifts and his heart. He liked to do for his woman, and he imagined that she would run if he spoiled her. Many women run from a man that seemed to be working too hard to get them. What they didn't understand was that some men genuinely wanted to give them the best.

"Aren't you handsome," Ijanay told him and smiled. She reached out her hand to shake.

He shook her hand and then kissed it. "You're looking just as beautiful yourself," he said and sniffed. "The food smells amazing." He then pulled a dozen roses from behind his back and handed them to her. "For you."

"Thanks, never a disappointing gentleman," she said and smelled them. "Nice, I hope you like fish. I've prepared salmon croquettes. Come on in. How about a glass of wine?"

"Perfect," Lex replied and stepped into Ijanay's home. The place was expertly neat just like her persona. The throw on the sofa looked thrown to perfection, and there was no sign that a kid lived there. That said a lot to him about her and the way she raised her child. He liked that.

"Here," she said and handed him a wine glass. "It's 2011 Esporao Monte Velho White. It cost just…"

"Eight dollars," he said and smiled. "It's perfect and can't believe you know about this one."

"Ah, ha. I know a little about wines and things, buddy. Let's head into the sitting area of the kitchen."

"Sure, let's do that," he replied and smiled. *Finally, I have met a woman with some class.*

26

At one a.m. Don Juan planned to be in the bar in an hour. The bar closed at two. He only needed an hour to scope the bar for a woman to take to a hotel and hold a business meeting.

Memories had slapped Don Juan hard as he pulled slowly onto Logan Street and parked a block away from Charlie B's. He looked around at the abandoned warehouses on one side of Logan and recalled the many thousands he had won playing dice on the abandoned stairs of one of the cribs. Another house was occupied by a squatter that he and his friends used to pull trains on hood-rat women looking for a variety of penises. Winos had drunk cheap Wild Irish Rose from the bottle on the stairs of another house. On the corner of Wayne Avenue and Logan Street stood Charlie B's on one corner and a Jamaican convenience store on the other. The store was more convenient to buy weed, not milk and bread. A commotion spilled out of the bar and brought him back from memory lane.

Money Shaker Monday at Charlie B's had brought the freaks out on a weekday. Amateur women were paid to shake what their mama's had given them, before thirsty men who spent their rent and child support money on them. With all that derriere floating around, Monday night was the perfect cover for Popz and Don Juan to meet and discuss how they were going to get that money together.

He lowered his stereo and turned the truck off as Popz, with his hand gripped around a naked woman's throat, pulling her out of the bar. He dragged her into the middle of Logan Street and slapped her with enough force that she slammed into a concrete staircase. Despite her deep caramel complexion, he had left a handprint on her cheek. Her eyes were clotted with blood. Her saggy breasts hung in the night air, and a skimpy thong covered her vagina, but not her ass, which was scratched from her fall.

"You a booty shaker, now, bitch," Popz yelled, and kicked her in the ass. "All for some fuckin' money, while my babies at the crib unsupervised by your crack-head-ass mother. You must be the fuck stupid."

Popz had venom dripping from his eyes, as he grabbed the woman's arm. "And you've been popping them fucking pills, too. Probably, around my kids, bitch," he barked and tossed her arm with force. "Shaking your ass for money to bang dope, huh?" he asked and counted money that he pulled from her panty line, the moment that he had snatched her from the bar top. "Two hundred and forty-six tax-free dollars. Good the fuck for you, whore," he said and pulled a lighter from his jeans pocket. He set the bills on fire and then threw them in her face.

Scrambling to her feet and screaming, the woman brushed the burning money from her body. "Why are you..." she began, before he kicked her in the back and forced her to slam into the hood of Don Juan's truck.

Don Juan hopped out the driver's seat and slammed the door loudly to announce his presence. "Popz, what's good, homie?" Don Juan asked, and checked his truck's grill.

Popz grabbed the woman off the truck and threw her into the street. "Nothing, 'bout to kill this bitch. I'll be in soon to rap to you."

27

By the time Popz entered the bar, Don Juan had a woman popping her pussy in his face. Charlie B's had stepped its game up, and he liked that. He poured another shot of Petron down the woman's ass crack and watched her ass cheeks clap, applauding him. His dick gave her a standing ovation.

"That's how you get down?" Popz asked parking in a seat next to Don Juan.

"Fo' sure," Don Juan told him. To the stripper, he said, "Put your number in my phone. I just came home, and I got some good dick for you." The woman followed his command, grabbed her boy-shorts from the bar and stepped off to the next man. "I'mma tell them I just got out of jail for the next two years." He smiled.

"Why not?" Popz shot back. "I've been here four years, yet I tell hoes I just moved here. Bust they ass every time. They love to think they're getting fresh dick."

Beautiful by Snoop Dogg featuring Pharrell blasted through the speakers, as the men realized that they had something in common. Both men were apprehensive about hooking up, but their pursuit of the almighty dollar drove them to do the unthinkable often. This meeting was no different.

"My bad 'bout the truck. There's a scratch on it," Popz said, attempting to pass Don Juan a thousand dollars.

"Dawg, I don't need your money for that. You did me a favor."

"By fucking up your wheel?" Popz asked perplexed.

"I'mma keep shit real, homie. Your baby mom, Saleena, got me booked, cuz."

"Don't call me, cuz, homie. Word?"

"Word. She lied and told my PO that I tried to kill her. She was my side piece and I had her and my girl pregnant at that time. They fought. Saleena loss the fight and me. To get back, she dug deep and low, and had me arrested."

Now Popz understood why Saleena had stared at Don Juan so interestingly. He had slapped her because he thought that she was eyeing Don Juan sexually. She was scared after learning that Don Juan was out of jail. She had probably seen her life flash before her eyes.

"I got a boy and a girl by her," Popz said. "I ain't know she was a dope fiend."

"I ain't gone kill her, my man. She's safe, just let her know, and this is no disrespect to you, if she disrespects me when I bust my gun next time, it won't be in the air to calm the situation."

Popz simply sipped his drink without responding. He had gotten the point and respected Don Juan's bold approach to the situation. He wasn't about to co-sign the threat. He was there to broker a deal and despite knowing Saleena had crossed Don Juan, Popz was about a dollar.

"You ain't got a job, yet?" Popz asked.

"Naw, I ain't looking to be an employee, homie. I'm trying to start my own business if you get my drift."

"How much start-up capital you need? You've been gon', you still have clients?"

"All I need is six months capital." The number of, if any, clients that he still had wasn't Popz business.

"Damn you want me to front a lot of dough, for a man fresh outta the joint. You know the going rate is $23,000-a-month," Popz said and knew that Don Juan understood that to mean $23,000 per kilo of cocaine.

"I don't need a handout."

"Oh, OK. Like that?"

"No doubt."

"Aiight. On the strength, I can loan you $130,000 for six months."

Don Juan's mathematical brain kicked into motion. Each kilo cost $23,000, so six joints totaled $138,000. Popz had shaved off eight grand. "Deal," Don Juan said, and shook Popz hand. Nothing mattered to him, things were bigger than Popz and his thoughts that he had done Don Juan a favor.

28

At 8:30 a.m. Tuesday morning, Don Juan didn't recall having hopped into the Range Rover, drove to, and parked in front of Trinity's school. Streets simply breezed by him and were full of continual green lights, absent STOP signs. Finally, he saw his ex-girlfriend holding the hand of his baby girl. There she was in a goose feather filled Dora the Explorer winter coat, matching book bag, and lunch box that Don Juan had bought her in New York City. He watched his scandalous ex-girlfriend kiss his precious daughter's forehead before she ran off into the schoolyard.

Don Juan spied Sherry stuffing her hands into her pockets and traipsed down Chelten Avenue along the side of Francis D. Pastorius Elementary School. Her home was a short two blocks away, leaving him ample time to secretly confront her about Rob, the undercover cop. How the hell did he infiltrate her life? Better yet, why? Did she know that he was an undercover cop? Was he in love with her, or was she an unknowing pawn in his plan to take down Popz? And most in need of an answer: How would this charade affect Trinity? It wouldn't as far as Don Juan Jackson was concerned.

Sherry reached the corner of Chelten Avenue and Ardleigh Street and crossed the intersection. She headed north on Ardleigh and looked into her cell phone. Dressed in dark clothing and gaudy sunglasses, Don Juan jumped out of his truck and hastily pursued her. She crossed the street and walked along a gate surrounding the parking lot of a Catholic church. She passed Stafford Street, and before she reached Price, he called her name.

Sherry spun around and recognized her child's father. She masked her panic, and boldly confronted him with, "So, what you a stalker now?" She had her cell phone held in the air, and said, "Nine-one-one is still available. I know you've been gone for six years, maybe you forgot."

"You got a smart ass mouth for a dumb bitch," he said and got deep into her face. "We really need to talk, Sherry. Now, and in private."

She pointed at herself. "Don, you and this bitch have nothing to talk about." She added a wicked smile. "And I really suggest that you don't come 'round here unannounced. This is bullshit. You asked me not to put the cops in our business, and I planned not to. But I may need a restraining order for this creepy shit." She stared into his eyes, visualizing a past that she had enjoyed, but she had long ago moved on. She needed too. Despite her having a genuine love for Don Juan, it was one based on her lack of self-esteem. She had since learned not to allow a man to walk over her because he was a good arm piece. No matter how good looking a man was, she had learned not to deal with him simply because she would be the envy of other women. And she would never settle for sharing a man to keep him. That was not acceptable. She had told him a lot through her eyes and spun around to walk toward her home.

Don Juan grabbed her with force and twirled her 180-degrees. He shoved his cell phone in her face, and said, "Your man is a fucking cop, Sherry. Just listen to this." He pressed play on his cell phone keypad, and for the millionth time, he replayed the threat made by Rob, the cop.

29

Popz had been on the basketball court at the Happy Hollow Playground shooting some early morning rounds. He used the jump-shots as a way to stay in shape and to keep his physique tight. When he was finished he sat on a bench and dug into his gym bag. He grabbed a bottled water, looked up, and Rob stood there.

"Where the fuck you come from? It's some thin air around this mutha fucka, I see," Popz said, opening the water. He took a big gulp and waited for the man in his space to reply. *And he had better give me one that made sense.*

"What's good, man? I want in on this money being made around here." Rob got straight to the point and took a seat.

Popz wiped his face with a dry rag and then took another sip of water. He wanted to backhand Rob off of the bench but decided against it. Knowing why he was approached in such a foul manner was something that he needed to know before the slap. "What gave you the balls to approach me with this? I mean you have a lot of guts man."

Rob opened his hand and exposed a badge. "Let's just get that out of the way."

"Oh, you're a cop? That's what's up." Unbothered. "I ain't got shit for you."

"Oh, you do. Let me break it down for you. Last night, Don Juan met you across the street at Charlie B's. At that time you offered him some drug weight and you're going to make sure that he gets it. You do that and the fact that you gave it to him never comes to the light or any other drug sales that I have you on. I am not looking to shut you down, but he has some old pals that we need him to reconnect with. He does that and we bust him and you go about your business. You got all that?"

"I do and I'm not with it. You want a water?" Popz asked, reaching into his bag. He pulled out a gun and jammed it into Rob's side. He looked him deeply in his eyes and then said, "I will kill your ass right here. Why are you fucking with me?"

"Put the damn gun away. You're not shooting anyone out here on the ball court sideline."

"See that's where you have the game fucked up. I will blow your brains out and pay all of the witnesses off." He stared very hard at the man before him, and then said, "Try me."

"Listen…" Rob began.

Rob was interrupted by Popz cocking his gun.

"Chill, man. I have a proposition for you. Just hear me out."

30

Lex had received an urgent text message from Don Juan and he immediately got into action. The message was vague, and he was asked not to reply. However, he trusted his pal and knew that he needed to make a move.

Lock's Philadelphia Gun Exchange carried the city's best selection of handguns, rifles, and shotguns. They carried all of the major manufacturers' pieces and could order anything that wasn't in stock. They even offered a layaway plan, but Lex didn't need that. What he needed were four Px4 Storm Inox Beretta pistols. Don Juan said that they had a major problem, so he went out to get major guns; one for each hand.

With him was a female friend that would apply for the guns and he'd pay for them. She knew all about the consequences of a straw purchase, but his money had convinced her to break the law. That, and he promised to pay her bail and hire an attorney for her if she was arrested.

31

The awestruck look splashed across Sherry's face was worthy of gracing the front cover of, I AM AN ASS MAGAZINE.

"How the hell could he do this to me? Of all the men, I could date, I get trapped by an undercover cop," she said as tears welled up in her eyes. She began to walk toward Chelten Avenue.

"Yo, Sherry," Don Juan yelled standing there. He looked confused. "Where are you going?"

"To get my baby. I can't believe this. I need to be near her and protect her."

"That's why I'm here, Sherry," he said, jogging after her. "Let me put both of you on a plane under fake names to wherever you want to go, and put you in a hotel suite. I'm not going to let this clown use you or my daughter to get at this Jersey cat, Popz."

"What the fuck, Don?" she asked violently. Tears aggressively poured from her eyes and she stopped walking. She slapped Don Juan so hard that she shifted his shades. "That's for cheating on me with that bitch." She slapped him again, and his shades flew off his face. "That's for letting that desperate bitch get you arrested and leaving me and Trinity alone." She huffed heavily as if she had completed a marathon.

Don Juan had love for her, too. He also hated her. Doing the right thing, he pulled her into his arms and then kissed her forehead. She rested her head on his chest and adored that she was still a tight fit there. He didn't resist comforting her; it was necessary.

"I miss you so much, Don Juan," she said and held him tightly.

He did not miss her and had no desire to pretend that he did. He was wise with no intentions of reigniting their young and immature love affair. But he would console her and value her as the mother of his daughter.

"You gotta gather yourself, baby. Where is he now?"

"He's supposed to be out of town, but maybe he's meeting with his fucking handler or some other crazy TV shit. I can't believe this, Don."

"Shit, neither the fuck can I. I'm gone take care of this, believe that. I just need you to follow my lead. You gotta leave Trinity in school and act as if I never told you this. You can't tell him, Sherry. All kinds of hell would break loose if you did."

"You gon' get the drugs for him?"

"What choice do I have? It's Popz or Trinity. When I meet the cop to pass off, that's when you and the baby gotta get out of here," he told her. "You gotta trust me. Can you do that?"

"Yes," she said as a car pulled over behind them.

They heard a car door slam and turned finding Rob hopping out of his Nissan Altima.

32

"So, this why I couldn't get no pussy last night?" Rob asked his fiancé. He pulled out his gun, and said, "You had to keep that thing clean and tight for this pretty lame. I should drop both of you mutha fuckas."

"No," Sherry yelled and walked over to him. "This is not what you think."

"Sherry...Sherry...Sherry. I see you not thinking, ma."

"He's dying, Rob. I'm sorry." She had both men dumbfounded. Hell, so was she.

"He gon' die this morning," Rob said and cocking his pistol.

"Please, Rob. Trust me, he ain't worth it. He has AIDS. He doesn't want me. He was having sex with boys in jail. He's gay."

"A fuckin' faggot," Rob said and chuckling. "I should drop you for that alone. What the fuck you crying for, Sherry? All of the pretty boys like him are fags."

"Because he can't be around for Trinity. She loves him."

Shit, Rob thought. *If I get my way, he won't be around Trinity anyway.*

"I'mma be out, Sherry. Sorry 'bout getting you caught up. I just didn't want to lose my child," Don Juan said and frowned. He had no idea that Sherry was so quick witted. She had crushed his manhood, but at the expense of assuring her daughter grew up with two biological parents. The grandparent custody battle flashed before Don Juan's eyes and he thanked God for Sherry's sharp acuity.

"Get your faggot ass outta here, you bitch boy, before I pop your top," Rob said smiling. He put his arm around Sherry, and said, "Come on, baby."

* * *

She rode shotgun in Rob's car, as he drove off the quiet Ardleigh and onto the busy Chelten Avenue. She pulled down her visor and began to clean up her face.

"Tell me I ain't the man," Rob said, bragging. He lowered the car stereo, and said, "I told you that he was a sucka for love, ass freak boy, and as soon as he had a chance, he was gon' holla at you."

"OK. OK. You were right. He actually believes that you're a goddamn cop."

"I laid that shit on him at Mommies."

"I know. He recorded it on his cell phone."

"What?" Rob asked. He was alarmed.

"Rob, make sure you take this phone. Confiscate it or whatever cops do," she said snickering. "He did tell me about Popz, too."

"Popz suppose to deliver him the coke, pre-cooked tomorrow around noon."

"Damn, we 'bout to be put on, Daddy," she said and ran her hand up his thigh to his dick. He immediately stiffened and she threw her head into his lap to please him.

33

At 9:44 p.m. Don Juan and Lex boarded a late night flight en route to Miami International Airport. By 12:39, they had landed, rented two Porsche Panamera, and checked into two poolside cabanas at the National Hotel on Collins Avenue.

A week out of jail, Don Juan was on his first trip to Miami, and staying at a $500 a night hotel room again. He settled into the room and then flipped through the hotel guide that listed all of the information about clubs, fashion, jewelry, and beaches. He was without luggage and had traveled as Don Juan Jackson. He had intended to bring out his alter ego on the Collins Avenue boutiques before the trip was over, though.

He sat the book on the table, walked to the sliding back door of the cabana, and found himself on a patio filled with furniture. He learned why the room was a cabana. The cabanas were lined with palm trees and a rectangular shaped pool that ran the length of the row of cabanas. Don Juan looked into the night sky and watched the stars shift across it. He stepped off the patio and crossed a sidewalk to the edge of the pool. He wondered had anyone jumped from one of the balconies into the pool. Noticing that the pool was only five-feet-deep, he hoped none. At the top of the pool, he recalled a makeshift stage there for Mariah Carey to perform via satellite for the 2005 MTV Video Music Awards. *One day, I'm in prison, and the next, I'm poolside at a Miami hotel.* Life was sweet and it would be sweeter if he could get the lame-ass cop off his neck, so he could raise his baby. For Don Juan, Trinity had been kidnapped and he planned to take every step to get her back.

Bright, but romantic lights beamed on the waves of the pool, under the night darkness. He leaned over the pool and saw his reflection in the water. With no one watching him, he made faces, while staring into the water. He chuckled at his own private joke; that carefree feeling of being alone and having fun with himself.

"Can I hear the joke?" the high pitched voice of a woman with a southern accent asked.

Damn, welcome to Miami, he thought. *Fuck the Miami Heat, this bitch is fire. You want a joke, ma, here you go:* "Let's see," he said smiling. "What kind of footwear does a spy wear?"

"You're really asking me a joke?" she asked, showing off straight white teeth, beneath cherry-red lipstick painted on full lips. She had a tanned coat sprayed on her flawless light skin giving her a tanned look. Sex appeal dripped from every pore beneath her cocktail dress.

"I am," Don Juan replied, smoothly. "You asked to hear a joke, and I am interested in pleasing a woman as beautiful as you are."

"Beautiful is such a bland word. That's comparable to me calling you handsome."

Don Juan had a charming sex appeal of his own that took charge of the conversation. "From what I can see you're beautiful. I'd have to get to know you there," he circled his index finger in the air around her right nipple, "before I describe you as otherwise." He had a swagger that had been on the inactive roster, but he was ready to get back in the game of flirting and dating. "So, can I get you to answer?"

"Cute for a thug. But because you've answered, I'll respond. I assume that there is running involved, and they have to be comfortable. I'd say Rockports or something like that."

"Final answer," he asked, furrowing his eyebrow like a seasoned game show host.

"You're too cute."

"Only cute? That's a bland word," he said, chuckling. "But the answer is sneakers."

She laughed lightly and a manicured hand covered her mouth.

Ah, the joy of first base, he thought.

"I'm Paradise," she said and held out her hand.

Boy, would I like to be in paradise? He held out his hand and shook hers. "Don Juan," he said, but wished he was Anwar at that moment.

"Come on. You're sexy and all..."

"Not as sexy and bodacious as you are."

"But you couldn't do better than, Don Juan. When did you take on that moniker? At the airport when you arrived, perhaps?"

Moniker, he thought. *An educated, sexy woman, huh?* Don Juan dug into his pocket, pulled out his wallet, and then flashed his ID in her face. "I've been Don Juan since 1981."

"OK, Mr. Jackson from Philly. Are you trying to grab a bite and a drink from the hotel bar?"

"You must be a local. Shame on you for trying to feed me and get me drunk to take advantage of me."

Paradise stepped deep into his space. She ran a finger down the side of his face, and said, "If I ever take advantage of you, your parents would know about it. And I'm from Memphis. Here on business."

"What kind of business?"

"Mine," she said, sternly. She smiled, and then said, "Just kidding. I'm into forensics, but we can talk about my career three months from now."

"Since I am sure that I'll be relevant at that time, let me lock up my room, and we can head out. Do you have a curfew?" he asked. Jogging into his cabana, his cell phone rang.

Don Juan answered the phone, as he dug in his suitcase for money.

Lex said, "She's bad, but we have a 6:30 flight out of here, so don't be out too late, homeboy."

"What? Lex, you're bugging, my dude. You see that ass. Her name is Paradise, and I've always wanted to go there. And I'm going while I have my chance."

"You're crazy as hell," Lex said. He was laughing.

"Besides, since we came here, I thought we had business to handle, and we were going to get at Popz a later date?"

"This is a part of the business, trust me," Lex said, seriously. "And Popz will get handled tomorrow as planned."

"Aiight, damn. I think I can be done with her by..."

"Four-thirty. We gotta be at the port by five. Oh, and be sure to record a cell phone diary of every place that you go, and use your pre-paid card, as well. Need a thorough record of where you've been for an alibi."

34

The next day, lunch was at McDonald's just off Chelten and Germantown Avenues. Trinity munched on a burger, fries, and a vanilla milkshake. The six-year-old was oblivious to the fact that her mother was a scandalous bitch, who had set out to take her father from her. Her biological one, anyway.

Sherry was transfixed on revenge against Don Juan. While he had served his time behind bars, she hatched the plan and had a good dummy to help her carry it out. She hadn't even put a battery in Rob's back, either. She religiously wrapped her lips around his penis and he gave her control. She had planned to slay Saleena, too, but the heroine was beating her so fiercely, she didn't warrant Sherry's wrath. Sherry plotted for the moment that she became good, sober, and clean before she gave Saleena what was due to her.

How senseless of Don Juan to believe that Sherry had no idea when he'd be released? How dare he not know that she wanted to pay his ass back for all of her pain and heartache?

Ignoring their daughter, Sherry asked her ex-boyfriend, "So, what're you going to do Don?"

"Come on, you know I don't bring my street shit home. That hasn't changed."

"I didn't know you were taking care of your home."

"Sherry," Don Juan said, and his cell phone rang interrupting him. She looked at him with glassy eyes.

"I know you're not going to answer that while we are talking?" she asked.

Six years ago that may have mattered.

Don Juan looked at her dementedly. He squinted his eyes and stared at her with a bitch-you-gotta-be-kidding look plastered on his face. He ripped his phone from his hip, and thought, *she has the audacity to ask me that when she got me in a position where I have to answer every call. She belongs to the cop, not me, so why would I care about respecting her. If Trinity was not involved, I would not give a damn about this lame ass cop.* Don Juan's interest in playing this cop's game was for the sake of Trinity Jackson. He just no longer cared about Sherry.

Point.

Blank.

Period.

"What's up, Paradise?" he asked, answering the phone. "I'm up in Fort Lauderdale with Lex. He's visiting his grandpa at a retirement community."

"Oh, how sweet?" Paradise replied. He wished that he could see her smile, at the same time, he loved the frown on Sherry's face. "So, you do want this pretty little phone back, right?"

"Of course, I do."

"Good. You do recall our deal?"

"I can only get my phone back in person."

"Right."

"And for the record, I'm getting my phone back tonight?"

"Good."

Sherry rolled her eyes and folded her arms. Don Juan said, "Paradise, lemme holla at you later, Baby."

"Paradise," Sherry said, as soon he hung up. "How many bills you drop in her panties at that strip club, Mommies."

"None," he said, and wondered: *How the fuck does she know about Mommies?* He pulled out another prepaid cell phone and called Popz. After he told him the meet spot, he hung up, and told Sherry, "It's showtime."

"What're you gonna do?"

He stood. "If I tell you, you may have to die, too." He then handed her the phone that Paradise had called him on and told her to keep it.

"Whose going to die?"

He kissed her forehead and told her to stop asking questions before he picked up Trinity and tickled her. She wiggled in his arms and cried with laughter.

He put her down and told her that he had to go.

"Dad, before you leave, I got another joke for you," Trinity said excitedly.

"Let me hear it, baby girl," he said and smiled. "I like to retell your jokes."

35

Popz had arrived at the JB Kelly School early to stake out the place. He needed to make sure that no one was there to rob him. He'd kill Don Juan if he saw anything out of place. That area of the neighborhood was typically quiet with huge homes, and perfect for the drug trade. He sat in his car when Rob walked up to the car and tapped on the window.

"What the fuck you doing here, man?" Popz was pissed and didn't know what to do. He was there early to stop any surprise and here he was in this predicament.

"Yo, don't you see what I am trying to do. I wanted to make you a proposal the last time that we met and you pulled a gun on me. Now I hope you see that I am pulling the strings here. Your boy Don Juan took the deal. He told me that he's meeting you here so I know that you have drugs on you."

"You'd be wrong. I was gone rob that sucka for his bread and tell him to kick rocks," Popz said and hoped that he was convincing. He was a great liar, but his encounters were with people that he was mentally superior. But this situation with Rob, the cop, was more than he could handle.

"So, you have a gun and drugs?" Rob asked, pulling out his gun. "I bet it's money in that duffle bag," he said, and reached into the window and pulled the bag out. With his gun trained on Popz, he opened the bag and saw money, as a car slowed as it came down Pulaski Avenue.

A tinted window rolled down and a gun extended out of the window. Bullets dance through the air and pierced Rob in four places. Popz ducked and tried to scramble out of the passenger side door to the pavement, but the car stopped and the shooter hopped out. He grabbed the duffle bag, tossed it in the car and pulled off. It was like they were out to kill Rob and take his drugs and money. *But why?* Popz thought and pulled off. *What the hell is going on here?*

36

Popz ran over the shot man with his truck and sped off southbound on Pulaski Avenue.

"What the fuck?" he yelled, pushing his truck through the Manheim Street red light. To hell with the SEPTA XH-bus about to cross and all of the commuters onboard.

He had spiraled out of control; a first for a seasoned street dealer that always kept his cool. He believed that he was being played by Don Juan, and knew, he should not have trusted him. Any man capable of getting his hands on as much cash as Don Juan so shortly after release from prison should have been handled more carefully. Greed had gripped Popz.

Without regard for human life, Popz raced through the Seymour Street stop sign as his cell phone rang. He grabbed it and saw the prepaid number that Don Juan had called him from. "Yo, what the fuck is going on, man? You set me up?"

"This shit is bigger than you. Are you shootin' down Pulaski?" Don Juan was calm, without a care in the world. Lex wouldn't have him any other way.

"Don't worry 'bout..."

"I don't give two fucks about him. You don't really know me, but you gotta trust me, though. Are you on fuckin' Pulaski?" Don Juan had bass in his voice.

Popz pushed pass Clapier Street, right through a street football game, and he didn't even beep. Angrily and with reluctance, he said, "I'm passing Abbottsford on Pulaski."

"Aiight, keep going down to Berkley and make a right, and then a sharp left onto Milne Street. About ten feet from the corner is a driveway. Pull into it and park in back of the only house on the right side with a balcony. Get out. Leave the keys in the truck, and walk out the driveway the same way that you came in."

Passing Zeralda Street, Popz approached Berkley, and said, "What kinda bullshit you on? I'm gonna flip a right and hop on the E-way."

"Yo, you just left a murder scene. You gotta get outta the truck. That clown, Rob, was a cop. And you can't out run them. He may have been undercover, and they could already have that vehicle. Park your shit. Walk down the driveway, and then down to Berkley to Wayne Avenue. Head up the steps to the Wayne Junction train station. Go across the platform to the Germantown Avenue side, and I'm parked right there."

"And then what?" Popz asked, pulling into the driveway.

"We gon' take care of business."

Popz had his own team and should've been on the phone with them, but Don Juan was persuasive. Under normal circumstances, he knew what was in store. *This is not normal*, Popz thought, walking down Berkley Street. The street was as steep as Steiner Street in San Francisco. He wondered, *what the fuck have I gotten into?*

37

Popz found himself on the run from a crime that he had not committed. But if caught, he'd be named a conspirator. He had come to Philadelphia and invaded Uptown for one purpose: money. Money from selling drugs, peddling guns, and having sex with as many women as possible.

Popz watched police cruisers zoom pass him, as he stood on the corner of Wayne Avenue and Berkley Street in front of an Asian owned deli and beer distributor. He pulled a Yankees fitted cap down over his forehead and concealed his face by looking downward. The light signaled from red to green and he dashed across the street heading south toward Wayne Junction.

Passing a mechanic shop, Popz heard his cell phone ringtone and it startled him. He was on edge. He gripped the phone from his hip and checked the caller ID. He flipped it open, and said, "What's up?" He was out of breath from the brisk walking.

"Where the fuck you at?" Don Juan asked. He was still calm.

"Going up the steps to the train station now." He held his breath because he was surrounded by the raunchy smell of urine and sex. He jogged around condoms and wrappers, evidencing the late night sex that took place on the secluded staircase under the cover of darkness. "Fuck."

"What happened?" Don Juan said concerned.

"Slipped on a damn pipe. Fucking crack heads."

"Man, come on." Don Juan hung up.

Popz slipped the phone onto the clip and continued to jog across the platform. Passengers boarded a SEPTA regional rail train, en route to the Philadelphia International Airport. The train conductor looked oddly at the thug running pass the train. He watched Popz until his head disappeared down the Germantown Avenue stairs.

* * *

At the bottom of the stairs, Don Juan was parked in a stolen Dodge Charger. Popz hopped into the passenger seat and Don Juan lowered the car stereo, as he pulled off.

"Let me get your cell phone." Don Juan demanded. Popz looked at him like a stupid person and Don Juan told him more sternly, "Pass the fucking phone."

Reluctantly, Popz passed him the phone. Don Juan drove with one hand and called his cell phone that he left in Miami with the other. Paradise did not answer. Don Juan redialed his phone again, and Paradise ignored the call. *Good*, he thought, holding down the button to lower the car window. Across from the Simon Gratz High School track, Don Juan snapped Popz's cell phone in two and tossed in through the passenger window and over a bridge.

"What the fuck are you doin?"

"That shit is a tracking device. Why you think I've been using these prepaid phones?" Don Juan asked, pulling up to the light at Germantown and Hunting Park Avenues.

"Rob took the drugs and someone rolled up and shot him and took it."

"Rob was a pig, homie. I knew that shit was going to be a setup."

"Rob ain't no fuckin' cop. He told you that bullshit?"

Don Juan flipped a right onto Hunting Park and told Popz about his encounter with Rob at Mommies.

"Dammit," Popz said and banged his fist against his knee. "He ain't no cop."

"What?"

"He got over on everybody. He set us up."

"How you figure that?" Don Juan was vexed. He had no idea what the hell was going on. He thought that he had all the answers, but he needed that question answered.

"He told me that you had the money and wanted me to sell you some bullshit dope. He must've planned to rob you for it because he told me he would sell it back to me for 25 G's."

"So, you were setting me up?" Don Juan was pissed. *And I planned to take care of this situation for you*, he thought. Just pass the Tasty Kake Factory, Don Juan swerved, parked across the street from a Catholic school, and whipped out his gun. He pumped a bullet into Popz's gut, and then another closer to his heart.

Popz scrambled for air. He clutched his stomach with one hand and his chest with the other. Nonchalantly, Don Juan reached over him and pushed the button to lower the seat.

Don Juan pulled into the traffic with a dead man lounged in the front seat next to him, as if nothing had happened.

38

Anger raped Don Juan of any sense of rationality. All of his pinned up heartache and anguish had surfaced. People were about to pay. He was tired of being screwed over. While killing Popz was a relief, he had scores to settle with some other people. To hell with being a nice guy. He always forgave and accepted one's apology. Things were great since his release, and he had hoped no one set him off like a bomb strapped to a martyr. He had planned to give out bad and devilishly deals. No more of the nice guy act. Rob had started the party and Popz had greedily invited himself. But Don Juan had other invitees that should be fashionably late to the party.

Cloaked in his suave and serene aura, Don Juan schlepped through the 30th Street train station and boarded a train for Washington, District of Columbia. His ticket had him going to Richmond, Virginia, but he would disembark in Baltimore, Maryland. He carried a briefcase and donned a blazer over jeans; a very casual passenger that just committed murder. He fiddled with an iPad, logging onto websites that involved Miami sightseeing. That didn't take murder from his mind. Popz was his first murder victim, but his emotional state confessed that it would not be his last. *Fuck everybody*, he thought as the train pulled into the Wilmington, Delaware station.

While the train stopped to pick up passengers, Don Juan confirmed that he, Anwar Muhammad, had an E-ticket awaiting him at Baltimore-Washington International Airport to board a flight back to Miami, Florida. He had murder on his mind, and thoughts of murdering Paradise in a lush bed at the National Hotel.

39

Lex posed as Sampson Orman and boarded a flight from Newark Liberty International Airport en route to Miami, Florida. He hadn't seen Don Juan since they had passed each other at the 30th Street Station and boarded trains in opposite directions. Both men would fair better if they only had to look out for themselves. Had they faced adversity while together, they could have both ended up in jail.

Lex had so much on his mind and he had not slept during the flight. His eyes had occasionally closed, and he watched reruns of two things: the crimes he had committed and the crimes that he had aided. After the quiet flight, he boarded a caravan marked with the

National Hotel's logo on the side. He watched palm trees and exotic cars pass by, as he headed to the hotel.

Upon his arrival, he headed to a cabana, flopped on the bed and flipped on the TV. He searched for a sense of normalcy. But he wouldn't get that. In a bad attempt to do so, he decided to call Ijanay. He had three missed called from her on his cell phone, which he had left in the hotel while he went back to Philadelphia for the day. Just after nine o'clock, despite knowing she'd be winding down to prepare for the next day, he gave her a call.

* * *

After a long day, there was nothing in Paradise's life but Don Juan kissing, nibbling and navigating his tongue all over her body. His hands and mouth were slowly roaming along her thigh. She hadn't even expected the bliss that sent chills through her loins. He used his thumbs to spread apart her wetness and feel the moisture of her spot. He grew harder and harder and was ready to penetrate her, but he planned to do so much more with his hands before he did that.

* * *

"I've tried to call you all day. That's so unfair of you to send me flowers from Miami and not take my calls. You knew I'd call to thank you," Ijanay said. She pretended to be upset but was smiling.

"Are you chastising me like one of your misbehaved students?"

"Of course."

"I like it."

She adored his sense of humor. It helped that she hadn't been showered with affection from a man in a long time. She said, "Thank you. When are you coming home?"

"I'm not missing anything, but you, of course. You understand that my job forces me to travel extensively."

"I do. And you're right, you're not missing anything, but two murders."

"What?"

"They found a man dead outside of John B. Kelley, so all schools received an alert to be ever vigilant for illicit activity near our schools. You'd think laws that enhance punishments for crimes committed within 1,000-feet of schools would deter it."

"No one cares about that."

"Or the man found burned to death in his own damn truck, and get this, he made a call to the police before he died," Ijanay said, catching Lex off guard.

"Enough about the news. When can I take you on a mini-vacation?" he asked, changing the subject.

"One day."

"Soon?"

"Maybe," she said after a brief pause, and then repeated, "Maybe."

"Fair enough."

Lex ended the call and raced out the hotel room. He had the valet bring his rented Porshe around and was directed to an Internet Cafe. He had to pilfer through the Philadelphia local news station's websites to ascertain what, if any, intelligence the police had to solve the murder that he helped conceal. He couldn't believe that he set someone on fire.

40

Thursday morning promised to be great for Federal Bureau of Investigation agent, Kwame Mason. After 9 a.m., he arrived outside the McCormick Jaguar Dealership. The peculiar luxury vehicle heist was boldly splashed across the Philadelphia Inquirer's suburban section; and, was quite the fuss on the morning news, despite the Christmas season buzz and a couple of murders.

Agent Mason, full of excitement, set off to investigate and solve that crime. The fact that thieves had posed as federal agents and stole a vehicle that Agent Mason could not afford, drove him mad. An African-American man was found shot twice, burned in a vehicle, and parked in Hunting Park. Another man was found shot execution style outside an elementary school. Those crimes were of no interest to Agent Mason. Jealousy had enraged him and he'd do whatever was necessary to put the unknown knaves in a federal penitentiary. It was a tall order for Agent Mason, who had never been the case agent of a fraud case.

Agent Mason had brought down white-collar criminals, but they were associated with drug organizations. He forced men that laundered money for drug dealers to testify at grand juries sitting in the Eastern District of Pennsylvania. He loved to harass the men that rented Bentley's and Aston Martin's to drug dealers willing to pay $2,000-a-month for the service and rode around able to showboat to their peers lying and telling people they had paid $300,000 for the vehicles. Agent Mason loved busting those idiots, as he often called them. He had no idea that he was in for a thriller, and would be mentally challenged. And if, he became too much of a thorn in anyone's ass involved in the Jaguar heist, he'd have a physical fight. He had foreseen the man responsible for the Jaguar theft as a weak and ineffectual fraudster.

Agent Mason found parking on trendy Conshohocken Avenue, a street in Bala Cynwyd lined with specialty and antique shops. They were all owned by Montgomery County's old money residents. The agent spied strollers driven by European-born nannies. This rich place was where very thought out fraudulent schemes happened. Everyone that visited the up-to-the-minute strip of boutiques was made of money. Had to be, there was no other reason to be there. Absolutely, no one believed a thug, obviously, an intelligent one posed as a wealthy man and had stolen from the old money. What drew the thieves there? There to exploit a rich woman. Did the knaves intend to mock and steal directly from the untouchables?

Agent Mason, and his solid 200-pounds hopped out of his government vehicle. He donned a cheap suit and penny loafers with quarters in them, as he jogged to the crime scene. This was no ordinary crime scene, though. There was no yellow crime scene tape. No witnesses milled about with their hearts set on jumping into the witness box to testify.

The wind was soft and delicate, a testament to a Philadelphia suburb wintry morning. Agent Mason entered the car dealership, however, prepared to heat things up.

41

Two days later, having arrived in Philadelphia shortly after ten a.m., Lex was taxied to the downtown Ritz Carlton instead of his northeast home. He did not want to be home. The reason was largely due to the absence of Desiree. He was accustomed to her presence. Despite her calling the police on him, he wanted her there. But he'd never admit that. His ghetto customs demanded that he fight his urge to get Desiree back after she had him arrested. Real men didn't stand for that or woman stealing from them. There he was with the Philadelphia Inquirer spread open, as he sipped Merlot at the 10 Arts Bistro, the bar in the Ritz's lobby.

He used the private time to watch business men ebb and flow through the hotel and that turned him on. He wanted to be a legitimate businessman. This integral part of American society was how he envisioned himself. White collar criminals worked, and they worked hard.

Lex recalled his adoptive parents speaking passionately about who worked harder. The man who brokered the deal to fund the twenty-story hotel? The architect that designed it? Or the man that ultimately built it? For Lex, the answer was a simple one. Hard work was convincing investors to part with millions. Without that the architect and contractor were irrelevant. Lex embodied white collar. He had a foxy smile on his face and asked the bartender for a refill.

Lex flipped to the suburb section of the newspaper and found the bold headline: THIEVES POSE AS AGENTS TO STEAL JAGUAR. The mastermind of the theft jumped from his seat and told the bartender to give him his check. He charged his drinks and appetizer to his room, and then hauled ass to it. The paper and the crap contained therein had to be consumed in privacy.

The elevator dropped him on the eighth floor. He was sweating like he had run there. He jammed his key into the door and sought refuge like he ran from someone chasing him. He turned on the TV and plopped on the bed before he started to read the article.

By the time, he reached the second sentence, he was interrupted by his cell phone ringing. He answered it after checking the caller ID.

Don Juan said, "Yo bro, some agent is on TV in front of the Jaguar dealer. He's investigating the theft of a Jag."

"So?" Lex asked nonchalantly. He couldn't let Don Juan hear any stress in his voice.

Despite his worry, he had a cool outer shell and never allowed his true position to show. He was a poker player at heart with no interest in anyone learning his true feelings. Emotional men should be dead according to him. He had total control over his actions no matter what triggered them. Bottom line, the agent had turned up the heat, but Lex planned to turn it off.

42

Don Juan had successfully forced Sherry to become a conniving, manipulative bitch. She had taken notes from the way he had screwed her over. Now she had men nibbling out the palm of her hand and doing whatever she wanted them to do. She had overheard him brag about being a pimp and she was pissed. After all, she had never sold sex and the John paid Don Juan. She had taken care of him and given him things as his woman and that had his labor under the delusion that he was a pimp. And because he lived under her roof and had access to her car, she felt that she was being pimped. For that, he deserved everything that she had set into motion.

By Sherry's estimation, Don Juan was a lame, pretty boy, and a wanna-be thug. She pleased him easily because he didn't require much. The things that he had pimped women out to do was small and meaningless to her. He was no real pimp. He was an attractive man able to capitalize on women who were without self-esteem and naive. They'd do anything to keep a man that was prettier than them.

Not Sherry.

She had bigger plans. Plans that involved pimpin' him, her baby's father. Why not con his emotions? Break him down to the lowest compound. If any bitch was capable of playing on his emotions she could. She had the one jewel that Don Juan worshipped: Trinity Jackson.

Gunz, Rob's homie, stepped into Sherry's crib and admired her body. Just after noon, she paraded around in panties and a bra. She was out to control and finally blessing Gunz with some sex would do the trick. The way she saw the situation, sex was the most effective tool to control a man.

Gunz plopped his thin, cut up frame on the sofa, and let his romantic eyes roam Sherry's curves. She had plenty. He tossed his Yankees fitted on an end table, revealing wavy hair. He sparked a blunt, and told her, "Come here, ma."

She walked to him and straddled on top of him. "Everything in those bags?" she asked, nodding her head toward the shopping bags that Gunz and brought in.

He kissed both her breasts, and said, "I haven't touched the money."

"You're sure that Popz doesn't know you."

"Don't even matter he's dead. He was found burned up in his truck."

She didn't let her emotion consume her. She maintained her composure although she was breaking down. She may have hated the man, but hearing of his death touched her. "Even better. Lemme see what's in the bag," she said, forcing back a look of worry. She masterfully hid her panic about learning that Popz was dead. Sherry was all about business. She let her panties drop to the floor, as she bent over in his face to rummage through the bags. He puffed a blunt and blew smoke between the crack of her ass. Gunz licked her clit from the back and ran his tongue between her ass cheeks to her asshole. His tongue circled around her hot spot and she jumped away from him. "What the fuck!"

"What's up, ma?"

"Gunz, you trying to play me? This money ain't the fuck real."

"What?"

She grabbed a handful of money and tossed it at him. *Is this man trying to play me?* Sherry thought. The bag was full of stacks of Benjamins showing on the front of the bills. The backs were blank. Her cell phone rang as she said, "This is some bullshit," grabbing the phone.

"They must have all been trying to play each other. And I bet Don Juan must have been responsible for killing Popz after I killed Rob. He was scrambling for cover and I didn't get him. But since I had the bag, I drove off."

Dammit, she thought, and said, "This Don Juan on my cell now. He better be talking what I want to hear. Or we're going to get his ass."

43

Don Juan raced his truck up the median of I-76. *Fuck the traffic. The hell with the state troopers who tried to get a handle on the three car pile up.* He had a daughter to save, and that was the only command that he obeyed.

"Pick up the phone you dizzy bitch", Don Juan said through clenched teeth over Lil Wayne blasting through the stereo. When she finally picked up, he said, "Yo, Sherry, you gotta go pick up Trinity. We got to get out of the city, ASAP." He had a sincere sense of urgency in his voice. He desperately wanted to save Trinity and Sherry would benefit by default. He accepted that.

"What? What are you talking about?" Sherry played dumbfounded, knowing his problem.

"Sherry, I'll explain all this shit on the plane."

"Plane? Do you realize that Rob is dead? I can't get on a mutha fuckin' plane and leave. The cops would lock my dumb ass up."

Don Juan hadn't thought of that. She was right, though. The detectives would make her a suspect if she was not in a state of mourning. His thoughts raced. He wanted Trinity far from any investigation and funeral. He needed to get his shit together before things further hit the fan. Had they left town together, the police would surmise that they had conspired and killed Rob.

"Listen," Sherry said. "Why don't you come over here and we figure this out together. You always trying to run shit, you don't know everything 'cause you from the streets."

"What the fuck you talking slick for? I'm looking out for the best interest of my daughter," Don Juan said as his other line beeped. It was Lex.

"This wouldn't be the fuck happening if you hadn't killed Rob," she said.

"Sherry, are you outta ya fuckin' mind. I ain't kill him. What the fuck would I kill him for? I'll be there in ten minutes. We gotta rap," he said, clicking over to Lex.

* * *

Sherry hung up the phone, looked in a mirror and smiled at Gunz. She said, "So, you know what you gotta do, right?"

"Yeah, now come here. I need to bust a nut before I kill your baby daddy."

44

When Don Juan parked in front of Francis D. Pastorius Elementary School, he took three minutes to locate his daughter in the schoolyard. Trinity stood in the middle of a group of girls playing jump rope. She was bundled in a coat with fur around the hood, but the sparkle of the diamonds that he had bought her caught his attention. His little mini diva was having a great time. She was larger than life and he loved that. Don Juan walked across the schoolyard.

He was ten feet away from his little girl when she yelled, "Daddy." She was excited and ran over to him. "What're you doing here? Where's my mom?" She was such a precious jewel and oblivious to the danger that she was in.

"We're gonna go get her now," Don Juan told her as he picked her up. He gave her a piggyback ride to his car and buckled her into the back seat.

"Daddy, can we get ice cream?"

"Ice cream? In this cold? How about we're going on a vacation for your Christmas break," he said, pulling into traffic. He didn't even sign her out of school.

"For real, Daddy?"

"Yup," he said and raised the radio volume to ponder about his next move.

Don Juan drove toward Trinity's home and wondered what his life would be if he reconciled with Sherry, and they raised Trinity in a married home. A vision so special that he thought to pursue Sherry romantically to get his way with her, but that changed as soon as he watched police detectives march up to her front door.

Don Juan drove right pass Sherry's home without being noticed. Trinity informed him that, he had passed her home. He told her, "We can't go get Mommy right now. The cops just went in there to ask your mom what happened to Rob, and we can't bother them. So," he said, looking at her in the rearview mirror, "we're going to get that ice cream."

"Ice cream. Ice cream." Trinity said, singing the words exposing her joy.

There was no reason to be joyful, though. At least not for Don Juan Jackson. There was no mistake that the same detective that had given the press conference in front of the police headquarters about the Jaguar theft was at Sherry's. What could they want with her? He had no idea and didn't plan on pulling up to her home as they questioned her.

Don Juan looked at Trinity and decided that he would hit the road. He was taking his daughter on the run with him without regard for Sherry's desires. If she was concerned, she would have gotten their daughter when he asked her to. He was the child's father and could take her wherever he pleased. At that moment, in the interest of Trinity, he decided to call Sherry.

The first time that Don Juan called, he did not get an answer. Then he called again, and Sherry answered.

Sherry said, "I thought you were on your way here. What's taking you so long? We gotta go get Trinity."

"I already have her."

"What?" Sherry said loudly. "What the hell are you doing with my daughter? You need to bring her here now."

"Why are you screaming? Who's there? Are you showing off?"

"Ain't no fucking one here," she said forcefully. "You killed my fiancé and I don't want you around my baby. Bring her here, now, Don Juan."

This bitch is setting me up, Don Juan thought madly, while not letting his daughter in on his anger. *I didn't even kill Rob, yet she's telling the police that shit. Stupid, bitch. She probably thinks I'd kill him to be with her. Fuck outta here, trick.*

"Listen," Don Juan said calmly. "I'm headed up I-95 to Friendly's on Cottman Avenue to buy Trini some ice cream. We will be there," he told her and hung up.

Don Juan was actually headed down I-76, nowhere near I-95, en route to the Philadelphia International Airport. He planned to take the next available flight out of the City of Brotherly Love and didn't care where he landed.

45

Lex was quiet, but an impressive downlow bully. He got the results that he wanted and didn't need to be in anyone's face for it to happen. But when he did, he always planned to shock and disrespect the receiver of his wrath. Certainly, his mother could help him with that delivering that. They were cut from the same cloth and it was strong cloth.

Lex arrived in Danbury, Connecticut and checked into a beggarly motel. No need for a fancy Ritz Carlton, if he intended to stay below the radar. Besides, there wasn't any three-star or higher lodging for miles, much less a Ritz Carlton. He was without bags and tired from the drive, so as soon as he entered the room, he kicked off his boots and lay down on the bed.

He thought about what he was responsible for with respect to him and Don Juan's experience over the past week. He hadn't expected Don Juan making the news, being blasted as a kidnapper and a murderer. Sadly, Lex knew who Rob's killer was, after all, he was on the scene.

While Don Juan had conducted his bogus drug transaction, Lex was parked on the corner of the block dressed in all black with his cell phone in the air recording. He had a female accomplice prepared to pull out in front of Rob, as he left the drug deal, causing an accident. That would have sparked the police to be summoned. The point was to force Rob to give the sexy decoy his true identity and other information to learn who he really was. Armed with that information, Lex planned to hunt down Rob—the police officer's—bank accounts and wreak havoc on them. Alas, things changed when a man hopped out his car and shot Rob.

Lex and the woman drove at a distance behind the man. They planned to follow the money and drugs to take them back. They drove as Lex called Don Juan to instruct him to get Popz before he left the area.

The mystery thug drove for two blocks, abandoned his vehicle, and Lex watched as he hopped into Sherry's.

Lex had to tell Don Juan that not only was his baby mama strapping him to the electric chair, but she was orchestrating the moves to send him there.

And now he had to see his mother to ask her what to do with all of this violence and drama that had taken over his quiet white-collar criminal lifestyle. He hoped that Don Juan was safe traveling in the meantime.

46

Don Juan looked over at his daughter. She was soundly asleep as the plane pulled into the gate at Chicago's O'Hare International Airport. He didn't want to wake her and was glad that he had no luggage. They were in first class and as soon as the plane's doors opened, he scooped her up and then deplaned. She was light; a relief because everything else in his life was heavy. He needed to think, and he couldn't do that with a daughter who fascinated about being in a new city after a plane ride, so he left her sleeping.

In the waiting area of the airport, he sat Trinity on a seat, sitting next to her. He tossed his hands over his face and shook his head. *What the hell am I going to do now? For all I know I am on the run and with a child. Fuck my life.*

The one thing that he knew he had to do was get Trinity's ice cream and a stable place to lay her head. He could only think of one hotel, and he was sure that they had high-quality ice cream.

* * *

After a half hour ride in the back of a taxi, Don Juan and Trinity were dropped in front of the Trump International Hotel & Tower Chicago. He remembered reading an article about Steve Harvey renting a penthouse there for $20,000 a month and figured that would be a great place to hide. No one would expect him to be in such a ritzy hotel. En route, he made a reservation on Expedia and had reserved a Grand Deluxe Lake View Two Bedroom Suite for $1,220.75 per night. He wanted Trinity to have her own room. To keep her from complaining or thinking too much about her mother, he planned to buy her toys and gifts to treat her and to treat her to a great time.

"Wake up, Trini," he said as the bellman opened the cab door.

She opened her eyes and looked at her dad puzzled. Trinity wrapped her arms around her dad and smiled. "Are we finally at your house daddy?"

"Yes, we are, baby," he said, grabbing her hand. He tipped the bellman $50 and then told his daughter. "Let's go see your new room."

"What about my ice cream?" she said, having not forgotten about that request.

"Coming right up. Vanilla and chocolate and I will even get you some brownies," he replied, walking into the hotel.

47

Bright and early the next morning, Lex was at the Danbury Federal Correctional Institute. He was checked-in by the corrections staff and then made to go through a metal detector before he was able to see his mother.

She came into the visiting room dressed in a two-piece tan uniform. Her long, curly hair hung low, and she had on a little mascara. When she got to where Lex sat, he stood and gave her a warm hug.

"You look beautiful," he said, smiling. "I miss you, mom." Although he had never had a moment with her that they weren't in a jail visiting room, he still missed and loved her dearly. They shared a bond that was special and unique compared to many other mothers and sons. He had no idea how much he was like his mother. What had she passed along to him?

"How are you, son?" she asked and had a seat across from him. They scooted their chairs closer so that only they could hear their conversation.

"I am OK, mom. But I have a serious problem as I told you on the phone. That's why I am here."

"Oh, that's all you came for?" she said, smiling.

"No," he said and chuckled. "You know what I mean, mother."

"I do, I was just joshing around. I need you to lighten up. I can see that something is really bothering you."

He leaned up, and said, "Do you want a snack." He then whispered, "I killed someone, and I need some advice on what to do about that."

"Do you now?" she said, furrowing a brow. "Who is someone?"

"Don Juan's baby's mother new flame. I burned that nigga up."

She frowned. "That's a lot."

"I know, mom. But he threatened my operation."

"You don't have an operation, son. That's first of all. Don't talk like that. You get money, but let's not paint you as running a RICO." She shook her head. "You got that?"

He shook his head, and said, "Mom, help me, please." He begged.

"Well, I have been in here working in this law library for fifteen years. I could defend a case better than Ben Matlock right now." She gave him a calm stare and then said, "Get your mom a pizza, ice cream bar, and a Pepsi. Together we will come up with a plan to get you out of that mess." He started to walk away, and she said, "That's if we can. I work magic. Not miracles."

48

TWO DAYS LATER

A vicious punch to the stomach forced Sherry to fold in half. She dropped to the ground and winced in pain. The gunman warned her repeatedly that she had better not scream or she'd never see her daughter again. She was dazed and looked around like she had seen two ghosts. Her head had hit the ground of her backyard hard, making her ears ring. She could barely hear out of her left ear, but she heard the man muffle something. She didn't move.

"Should I kick her in the face? Maybe she will move to the pool," the gunman asked his masked accomplice, pulling his leg into the air.

"No," he said, grabbing her. He raised his mask, and asked, "Why would you set me up like that, Sherry. After all that we have been through. And to think that I was going out of my mind to protect you from that clown."

"Why you take off ya mask?" Lex asked Don Juan. He was pissed. They were in an alley. Someone could have walked by and reported that they were assaulting a neighbor.

Why the hell did he take off the mask?

"Sherry," Don Juan said, tossing her into an inflatable pool with dirty rain water in it. "It's crazy that you would do this to me when I have always tried to look out for your best interest and definitely be a great dad to our daughter."

"Where is my baby?" she asked. She didn't care about anything else. She was whimpering.

Don Juan shot her in the mouth.

"Stupid bitch," he said, and then spit in her face. "That's none of your fucking business."

He could not take it any longer. His anger had brewed prior to getting there and her audacity to ask about their child while not answering his question had forced him to snap.

"That's why I took my mask off. I knew I was going to eliminate any witnesses." He looked at the stars above, and said, "She was a witness."

49

Federal Agent Mason felt the tides turning and not in his direction. He sat at his desk and watched the footage of Gunz hopping into Sherry's car after shooting Rob. Someone had sent a CD to him via express mail. He pressed his index fingers into his temples and massaged them. He could strangle himself, for being so dumb. He let a woman play him and that killed him. He rewound the tape and watched it again. And then, again.

His partner would be disappointed in him if he told him about the tape. He concealed it in his bottom desk drawer and sought to get a warrant to search Sherry's home for evidence of a crime. He sent an E-mail to the Assistant United States Attorney assigned to this case and then shook his head. This was his second case as the lead and it was a tangled mess. *Sherry and her pal are going down*, he thought as he stuffed his gun into its holster. He was going to arrest Sherry and he hoped that she resisted.

His partner walked over to his desk, and said, "Where are you headed, man? We have a serious problem?"

Tell me about it, he thought, and then said, "What's happening now?"

"I will explain on the way. But we have to get over and interview Sherry again. She fingered her boyfriend, Don Juan for killing her new boyfriend, but I am not convinced of that anymore. She needs to come up with some new answers." He continued to speed walk out of the office, hoping what he said was enough to give him the opportunity to figure out the rest of his lie.

50

"Excuse me, gentleman," Agent Mason said, walking up to a police barrier on Price Street. He stood there, staring at Sherry's home and Philadelphia PD walking in and out. His mind whirled with thoughts of his own family as he envisioned Sherry and her daughter dead.

"Mason," PPD Sergeant Dorsey called. "What a surprise. And welcome to this cluster fuck." He signaled for the officer guarding the barrier to allow Mason and his partner onto the street.

"What do you have?"

"Why are you here? First." The sergeant had a cute sneer on his face.

He turned, squinted into the fresh air, and nodded towards the house.

"I'm here for Sherry," he said. "She's a witness of mine. I was coming to chat with her."

"You're a bit late for that. She's dead'er than Elvis."

"Any leads on the perp?" His case had just become more complicated.

"So far just that there was one gunshot. An older, ex-military man thinks it may have been muffled like it was shot from a gun with a silencer. Two masked men were seen running from the scene. I mean, you can imagine that there's no one with home cameras around here. But I do have an officer canvassing for it."

"Where's the daughter? She has a six-year-old," Agent Mason replied, moving towards the home, already compartmentalizing.

"Well, she's with the father and has been for two days. Against the mother's wishes by the way. They went on a vacation to Chicago without her permission. Neither of them has legal custody."

"Sherry was alive when you got here?"

"No."

"So you know the girl is with the dad, how?"

"Gossip from a neighbor. Apparently, the walls are very thin and she eavesdrops as part of her religion."

"Yes, a commandment. Thou shall not miss any dirt on your neighbors," Agent Waverley said, frowning.

"Yeah, you know how these people love to gossip," Agent Mason said. "I wonder what else she knows."

There was a long pause before he said, "I'm assuming you want my source?"

"Of course," Mason said.

"No problem," Sergeant Dorsey said. "But I applied for the bureau, and looking forward to your recommendation." He winked.

Mason kept his voice steady. "Sure. Now, what's her name."

51

Hours had passed and not once had Don Juan picked up the phone. He had taken an Amtrak train to Pittsburgh, Pennsylvania. After a one-hour layover, he boarded another Amtrak train. Nine hours and forty-six minutes later, he was back in Chicago. A five-minute cab later, he was at the Trump International Hotel and Tower.

"Daddy...Daddy," his daughter yelled as the door closed behind him. He wore a frown on his face, although he was glad to be back with his daughter and that she was safe.

He handed her roses and gave her a hug.

"Thanks, daddy," she said. After examining them, she said, " Why'd you buy me flowers?"

"Yeah," Monica said. "You didn't get me any flowers."

He had a seat at the desk and stared out of the window. His gaze went out into Lake Michigan pass the Navy Pier Ferris wheel.

"Well, mom. I brought you here to make up for some lost time."

"Yet, you've been gone nearly a whole day."

"I know," he said, pulling his daughter into his arms, and then onto his lap. He kissed her forehead, and said, "There's been an accident, mom." He froze.

He had been forced to deal with the agony of knowing that he had to explain to his daughter that her mother was dead. What was he supposed to say? Was there a correct way to do this. Naturally, he wanted to shield her from any kind of pain, but he was the person to tell her about her mother. He let a tear fall from his eye. He had to because no child was ever too young to know about their parent being killed, so he had to man-up and do it.

"Are those tears?" his mother asked.

Should I lie about how this happened? Will the media and police questioning be overheard by her when we get back to Philadelphia? If we go back? He desperately wanted to protect her from this. He was angry at himself for not thinking about the impact his kill would have on his child.

"Why're you crying, daddy?" She was wiping his tear away and started to tear up herself. She wrapped her little arms around his neck, locking her tiny hands together at the back of his neck.

Pulling her back, he looked back and forth between his daughter and his mother. His mother had moved closer to him and had her hand on his shoulder.

He counted in his head. When he was at ten, he said, "Your mom...your mom. She has died. Someone killed her and Rob. I saw it on the news and everyone knows. Lex called and told me, too. The police are investigating and looking for the killer, baby." He pulled her closer in his arms as more tears began to fall from his face as he watched his daughter's face fade deeper and deeper into sadness. *What the fuck have I done.*

She was speechless. His mother was equally silent. That was good because he had no answers. Trinity rested her head on his chest. He didn't know if she was crying. He was scared to look at her face to even find out. Would she be able to read on his face that he was the killer?

For five minutes they just sat there. All of them quiet.

Finally, he pulled Trinity off of his chest and looked at her, and said, "Are you OK?"

"Yes, daddy, I don't want to cry and make you mad. I have to be a big girl."

You're such an idiot, man. What the fuck were you thinking? Now what? Your daughter has no idea what the fuck is going on. But when she does this will all hit her like a ton of bricks and it'll be all your fault.

He said, "Mom, pack our things, please. We have to go back to Philly tonight."

52

When Don Juan walked through the jetway, he was carrying Trinity who was asleep in his arms. His mother was behind them, carrying a duffle bag filled with cash and rolling a carry-on bag. They walked into the Delta Airways waiting area and weaved around other passengers to get out of the Philadelphia International Airport.

Just as they began to walk through the security gate, they were accosted by three men in suits. Behind them, a man in plain clothes with a Philadelphia PD badge around his throat stepped out of the shadows.

"Mr. Jackson..." Agent Mason said, wearing a classic sneer.

"Yes," Don Juan said calmly.

"Hand your daughter to your mother. We have a problem and we need you to come with us."

"Have you found the people responsible for…"—he paused to look at his daughter to be sure that she remained asleep—"…killing my baby's mother?" He whispered with venom in his tone.

"We're looking at him," the PPD officer said. "No way you thought that you were going to walk through *my* airport and back into this city like nothing happened."

"What?" Don Juan said defensively. "What the hell are you talking about?"

"Yeah, we've been in Chicago," Don Juan's mother said.

"Look put the baby on the floor, and we can discuss at the FBI HQ," Agent Mason said. "Don't make a scene." He hadn't even realized his hand had dropped to his pistol. His thoughts were jumbled and breath bottlenecked in his throat while he processed what he would do if Don Juan didn't comply.

Don Juan stood there speechless, glancing into the sea of travelers to see if undercover armed men waited for him to make a bad move. *What the fuck are they doing here*, he thought. *This is some pure bullshit. Lex must have ratted me out. No one else knew I'd be here.* Reluctantly and shaking his head, he shook Trinity awake.

As she gathered her senses, Don Juan told Agent Mason, "Do not handcuff me in front of my daughter."

"I can do that."

"And am I under arrest?"

"No, but undoubtedly you understand that you are her de facto boyfriend and no doubt our number one suspect."

"For now, at least," his mother said.

"Yeah," Don Juan said. "I was in Chicago three days."

"Could be an alibi or could be misdirection. But we will discuss that at HQ."

Don Juan sat Trinity on her feet and she clung to his pant leg. He bent down, meeting her face with squared shoulders, and asked, "You're a big girl, right, baby?"

She shook her head while looking around at all of the men.

"OK, Daddy has to go and speak with these men about Mommie, OK. You have to go with grandma." He could see the pain begin to spread across her face. "You said you're a big girl so no crying and pouting. She's going to take you to another big hotel downtown. You want to go to the Ritz Carlton for truffle fries and ice cream?

"Yes," she said without excitement.

"OK, good. Give me a hug." They embraced and he looked his mom in the eye. "Check into the Ritz for a few days. I will be there later on tonight." He nudged Trinity towards his mother who grabbed her hand and began to walk away.

"Now let's get this scumbag…"

"What's your problem?" Don Juan said to the PPD officer. "Take notes at how professional the feds are. You're being an ass and child's mother is dead. And now you mutha fuckas wanna question me like I am a damn suspect. I bet her boyfriend is roaming free while harass me."

He knew that be a lie, but he was giving the performance of his life. Tony Award worthy.

"I'll like a call to have my lawyer meet us there," Don Juan said, frowning. "I guess I am ready."

* * *

Five hours later, Don Juan walked out of the downtown FBI Office—his attorney by his side—with the caveat that he wasn't to leave the area sans permission. Apparently, he remained a suspect in the murder investigation of Sheryl Hartman.

"Hey," Mason yelled to Don Juan's back just as he cleared the building's doors.

Don Juan thought about running. Where would he hide immediately ran through his head? He was in the middle of the fifth largest city and he wouldn't have gotten far on foot. So he had to hide right under their noses. But where? After making it out to the Arch Street pavement he stopped.

The agent said, "You were eloquent in there and your alibi looks very neat and tidy, but..."

"Here we go," Tamara Macintosh said. She was Don Juan's attorney, and the mother of stripper, Roneeka Macintosh. "The interview is over, Agent Mason."

Ignoring the lawyer, he said, "I want you to know that the minute your story unravels, I will be putting the cuffs on you myself."

Don Juan smirked and opened his mouth to reply, but was stopped by his layer.

"No, it's OK," Don Juan said to his lawyer. To the agent, he said, "Good luck with that."

Epilogue

ONE YEAR LATER

The sun was in the room when he woke. Sleep was never easy.

Don Juan sat up and looked at the window. The curtains were flapping wildly. He had fallen asleep with the windows wide open. In his new digs, he could do that. He lived in the Santa Monica area of California in a condo full of life, sunshine, and peace. He was a single, dating man, but he wasn't alone. His daughter, Trinity lived with him and attended nearby John Muir Elementary School.

She had adjusted to the school and new area, and although she didn't mention her mother much, Don Juan had caught her staring in space a few times. Moments that he had assumed she may have been thinking about her mother. School counselors informed him that she may be coping with the loss through silence and one day the death may hit her and she'll have a breakdown. He hoped that she didn't. Killing him most about the murder of Sherry was the effect that it would have on his daughter. That was about all of the guilt that he had. When he was released from prison he vowed to get revenge on the one person who put him there. No, he didn't expect that to come in the form of death, but it had, and he was without remorse. Except as it related to Trinity.

He hopped off the bed, opened his bedroom door, saw his daughter there, fresh out of the bathroom, and fully dressed. He walked to her and put his hand on her head. He shook it.

"How's my wonderful daughter?" he asked.

Moving her head, she replied, "Don't touch my hair, Dad."

"Oh, I forgot. You're a big girl."

"Yes. Woman of the house, right?"

"Yes, ma'am." He considered his comment and hoped that he was teaching her the right things because as a single dad, having murdered her mother was taxing on his parenting skills. He didn't know how gentle to be or how much he should let her grow up.

"So, I have my show-and-tell ready. I can't wait to get to school after breakfast. I am ready to show off my rabbit," she said, pointing at the small rabbit in a cage that was perfect for her to easily carry.

"OK," he said, walking towards the kitchen. "Cereal or—"

"Waffffflllleeessss," she sang.

"OK, let's do it," he said, racing to get his ringing cell phone. He answered, and said to the caller, "You're on your honeymoon, why the hell is you calling me."

"Just checking in," Lex said on the other end of the line. "I'm safe no one followed me."

"This paranoia you have has to stop. Everything is a done deal, man. I am officially cleared of any wrongdoing."

"Yeah, thanks to this dick I have been giving to your lawyer. I told you that she would come in handy."

"Where the hell is Ijaynay because you're talking like you're not in Cancun with your new wife."

"In the shower."

"OK, good. Join her, man, and enjoy your honeymoon. Now, I have to go. I have to prepare my daughter for school." He hung up and turned to Trinity. "Now where were we," he said, smiling.

Life couldn't be better.

Rahiem Brooks Biography

The Fiction Work:
"My previous novels explored how people were tied together by crime," Brooks says. "But with A Butler Christmas, I sought to connect people by the mystery of falling in love with new friends and estranged family. I'm excited and eager and anxious—like going on my sophomore dance. To join the Prodigy Gold family is a great honor and thrills me to my wing tips."

The Non-Fiction Work:
"I am very excited to give back to the writing and publishing communities with my short publishing tips. Everyone publishes tomes on the topic and many people get discouraged with respect to employing effective and traditional publishing tactics because of the vast amount of material out there. I've decided to do small essays that people can act on and have a clear understanding of it because I explain in detail with examples." Brooks can be reached for questions about publishing, consultations,

and speaking engagements at rbrooks@prodigygold-books.com.

The Career Story:
Rahiem Jerome Brooks is the breakout novelist and is a member of the Mystery Writers of America. His debut thriller, LAUGH NOW won 2010 African-Americans on the Move Book Club's (AAMBC) Book of the Year & he earned 2011 AAMBC Author of the Year. LAUGH NOW also the Most Creative Plot at the DMV Expo's Creative Excellent Awards. Rahiem was also nominated at the 2011 & 2012 African-American Literary Awards for Mystery of the Year for Con Test and Murder in Germantown.

The Background Story:
Brooks grew up in Philadelphia before trekking to Los Angeles to study film/TV at UCLA. Finding it difficult to break into Hollywood, he adapted his screenplay into his first novel and later pursued an English degree at Harvard University and making writing a full-time job. He lives in Philadelphia with a Manx.